THE BIRTHDAY PARTY OF NO RETURN!

GOOSEBUMPS®
NOW WITH BONUS FEATURES!

NIGHT OF THE LIVING DUMMY

DEEP TROUBLE

MONSTER BLOOD

THE HAUNTED MASK

ONE DAY AT HORRORLAND

THE CURSE OF THE MUMMY'S TOMB

BE CAREFUL WHAT YOU WISH FOR

SAY CHEESE AND DIE!

THE HORROR AT CAMP JELLYJAM

HOW I GOT MY SHRUNKEN HEAD

THE WEREWOLF OF FEVER SWAMP

A NIGHT IN TERROR TOWER

WELCOME TO DEAD HOUSE

WELCOME TO CAMP NIGHTMARE

GHOST BEACH

THE SCARECROW WALKS AT MIDNIGHT

YOU CAN'T SCARE ME!

RETURN OF THE MUMMY

REVENGE OF THE LAWN GNOMES

PHANTOM OF THE AUDITORIUM

VAMPIRE BREATH

STAY OUT OF THE BASEMENT

THE BIRTHDAY PARTY OF NO RETURN!

R.L. STINE

SCHOLASTIC INC.
New York Toronto London Auckland
Sydney Mexico City New Delhi Hong Kong

No part of this publication may be reproduced, stored in a retrieval system, or transmitted in any form or by any means, electronic, mechanical, photocopying, recording, or otherwise, without written permission of the publisher. For information regarding permission, write to Scholastic Inc., Attention: Permissions Department, 557 Broadway, New York, NY 10012.

ISBN 978-0-545-28938-2

Goosebumps book series created by Parachute Press, Inc.
Copyright © 2012 by Scholastic Inc.

All rights reserved. Published by Scholastic Inc., *Publishers since 1920.* SCHOLASTIC, GOOSEBUMPS, GOOSEBUMPS HORRORLAND, and associated logos are trademarks and/or registered trademarks of Scholastic Inc.

12 11 10 9 8 7 6 5 4 3   12 13 14 15 16 17/0

Printed in the U.S.A.   40
First printing, April 2012

WELCOME TO THE HALL OF HORRORS

THERE'S ALWAYS ROOM FOR ONE MORE SCREAM

Welcome. Come in. You have found the Hall of Horrors.

Don't look so frightened. Or maybe you *should* look frightened. After all, we don't sell ice cream or popcorn here. We don't hand out cheery balloons.

This old castle is where the darkest, scariest stories are kept.

Come into the Unliving Room.

Just step over that giant boa constrictor. Don't worry. He almost never strikes when he's curled up like that. Besides, I fed him someone — oops — I mean, *something* this morning.

The Hall of Horrors is a very special place.

Frightened kids find their way here. Haunted kids. Kids with terrifying stories to tell.

They are eager to tell their stories to me. For I am the Listener. I am the Story-Keeper. I keep the stories safe within these castle walls.

1

We have a visitor today. His name is Lee Hargrove. He is twelve.

Lee is all tense, hunched up in that big leather harmchair. And what is he squeezing in his hand? Is it a rabbit's foot?

Let's ask him.

"Why did you bring that rabbit's foot, Lee?"

"Because I've had some bad luck lately. I hope this is a good-luck charm."

"Well, it wasn't good luck for the rabbit!" I joke. Lee doesn't smile.

"When did your bad luck start?"

"I guess my worst luck was at my friend's birthday party. It was a horrible day for me. Things got totally out of control. And I was asked to leave the party."

"Why don't you start at the beginning, Lee? I am the Story-Keeper. Tell me your story."

Lee squeezes the rabbit's foot in his fist. "It's a creepy story. Are you sure you want me to tell it?"

Go ahead, Lee. Don't be afraid. There's Always Room for One More Scream in the Hall of Horrors.

1

My name is Lee Hargrove, and I want to start out by saying that Cory Duckworth is my friend.

It's true that I *hate* Cory a lot of the time. But that's only because he is so lucky. Cory is lucky *all* the time. I mean, twenty-four hours a day and on weekends, too.

That's why a lot of kids at Garfield Middle School call him Lucky Duck. (Duckworth — get it?)

Cory even *looks* lucky. He has curly blond hair and round blue eyes, a nice smile, and a dimple in his chin. You know. The kind of cute dimple that says *I'm luckier than you.*

Cory is smart and has a funny sense of humor. And he's really good at sports. Which is another reason why I hate him.

See, I'm into sports, too. And I have a goal. I guess you could call it my one big dream in life.

All I want is a scholarship to Summer Sports Camp.

It's only spring. But I think about it all the time. Summer Sports Camp is very expensive. My parents are both teachers at the high school. They say they can't afford it.

So I need a scholarship.

I don't want to hang around the house playing the same video game over and over like I did last summer. Some awesome pro athletes teach at the camp. I have to be there. I have to meet them.

Can I get the scholarship? There are only a few things in my way. And most of them are Cory Duckworth.

See, Lucky Duck is trying for the same scholarship. And so is Laura Grodin. Laura is twelve like us, and she's in our class.

Some kids say I have a total crush on Laura, and they may be right.

Cory, Laura, and I, and a bunch of other kids are trying out for the scholarship. I know we three are the best. But only one kid can win it from our school.

That means Laura and I are competing against one of the luckiest dudes in the universe. How can we defeat that dimple? Those sparkling blue eyes? That winning smile?

It won't be easy. We have to compete in three different sports. And none of them is my best sport. But we also get judged on sportsmanship

4

and improvement and desire. And I plan to win at ALL of those.

I'm going to do whatever it takes. I'm serious.

After school, I was walking down the crowded hall to my locker. Lots of kids were heading to the soccer field. See, our soccer team, the Garfield Gorillas, plays in a spring league.

I ducked under the low yellow and blue banner: GO GORILLAS.

And suddenly, someone was waving something under my nose. I pulled my head back, and I saw it clearly — a twenty-dollar bill.

Yes. Lucky Duckworth was crinkling a twenty-dollar bill in my face. And he was flashing me his toothy grin.

"Check it out, Lee," he said. He rubbed the money on my cheek.

I tried to jerk my face away. "What's up with that?"

Cory danced away a few feet. He never walks. He dances or he struts or he shuffles and slides.

"Remember? I found this money in the lunchroom?" Cory said. "Well, guess what? I turned it in to the principal's office. But no one claimed it. So I get to keep it."

"Lucky," I muttered.

Typical, I thought to myself.

That's a perfect Cory story. I guess you're

starting to get the idea. He doesn't need a rabbit's foot for luck.

Cory danced off down the hall. I stuck my head in my locker and screamed for a minute or two. I wasn't angry or upset. Really. Sometimes it just feels good to scream.

I mean, Cory is my friend. I can't get angry when good things happen to him — right?

I pulled my head from the locker and gazed down the hall. Laura Grodin was leaning against the wall, talking to Cory. She kept running a hand through her straight red hair and blinking her green eyes at him.

He was flashing the twenty-dollar bill in her face. And bragging about what a good finder he is. I heard him say he could sniff out money from two blocks away.

Ha. Guess he also plans to sniff out the scholarship money that I desperately need.

I watched him showing off to Laura. And I thought: *I don't want anything bad to happen to Cory. I just wish there was a way to borrow his good luck for a while.*

Cory and Laura walked off together. I saw Mr. Grady, a school janitor, up high on a ladder in the middle of the hall. He was reaching both hands up to replace a ceiling light.

Cory and Laura stopped at one side of the ladder.

Mr. Grady had the big metal light fixture in

both hands. What happened next seemed to move in slow motion.

The janitor let out a cry. I saw the heavy fixture slip from his grasp.

Laura was talking to Cory. She didn't see it fall. It was going to crush her head.

I opened my mouth in a horrified scream.

Cory spun around and caught the light fixture —
inches above Laura's head.

Laura toppled back against the wall. Her red
hair fell over her face. She uttered a startled gasp.

"Whoa." On top of the ladder, Mr. Grady shook
his head. "Great catch, kid."

"Just lucky," Cory said. He flashed the janitor
a grin.

Laura brushed the hair from her eyes. "Cory,
you — you saved my life," she stammered. "I
mean, really."

Cory smiled and flashed his dimple. "Just a
lucky catch," he said. He handed the light fixture
up to Mr. Grady.

I couldn't help it. As I watched Cory and Laura
walk away, I had a few bitter thoughts.

Mainly, I thought: *Why didn't I get a chance to
make the catch and impress Laura? How does
one guy get to be so lucky?*

*　　*　　*

After school the next afternoon, Coach Taylor called basketball practice. The team plays in late fall. But he likes to get a lot of spring practices in to keep us in shape.

I usually play center and Cory is a forward. That's because my defense is better than his.

Basketball is actually my best sport. Partly because I'm tall and lanky. I'm almost two inches taller than Cory.

Too bad it isn't part of the scholarship competition. The competition sports are tennis, bowling, and football.

But Coach Taylor said our game today was a good warm-up. He said he'd be watching us. Getting an idea of who to keep an eye on.

So the pressure was on. I wanted to look good.

We all dribbled around a bit. Pale sunlight drifted down from the high gym windows.

Some kids hung out at the wall, watching our practice. And I saw some men in ties and dark suits. Two of them wore blue baseball caps.

Coach Taylor waved us over. He's a young dude with very short brown hair and a two-day brown stubble of beard on his cheeks. He wears glasses, and he's short and not very athletic looking.

We think this might be his first job after college. I mean, he almost looks like a teenager except for the stubbly beard. But he's a good guy and a good coach. We all really like him.

"Divide up. Two teams," he said when we gathered in front of him. "Work hard, guys. Do your best. We've got some people here watching you today."

He motioned with his head toward the three tall, serious-looking men leaning against the far gym wall. Then he blew his whistle, and we ran out to play a game against each other.

We played hard. It was more intense than a regular practice.

I didn't know who those three guys in suits were. But Coach Taylor seemed to think they were important.

I kept glancing at them during our game. They were giants. I mean, like, seven feet tall. And big. Maybe they were athletes.

Cory and I played on different teams. On defense, we guarded each other. I was having a good game. Cory was having a hard time getting around me.

I stole the ball away from him once. And I messed up a couple of his shots. I was really getting in his face.

But near the end of the game, he got lucky. Big surprise — right?

I saw him coming. He was driving the ball right down the court, coming directly toward me.

I know his moves. He was going to drive straight at me. Give me a fake to the left. Then when I went for the fake, he would swerve around me to the right and take it to the basket.

I'd fallen for that move a lot of times. But not today.

I tightened my leg muscles. Rooted myself to the floor. Stuck my arms out.

He was coming on fast. Pounding the ball on the floor as he ran toward me.

I stuck my arms out farther. *I'm a wall*, I thought. *I'm a wall. You can't get through me.*

"Hey!" I uttered a cry as pain shot over my eye.

A bug. Some stupid bug flew into my eye. My eye throbbed.

I ducked my head. Tried to rub the bug away.

But it only made the pain more intense.

Cory came to a hard stop in front of me. He arched his arms — and sent a high layup right over me.

Please, please — don't go in! I prayed. *Don't go in!*

Don't make me look like the biggest loser on the floor.

Please?

3

Chinnng. I heard the ball hit the rim of the basket. *Swoosh.* I heard it go through.

Cheers rang out.

I rubbed my eye with the back of my hand. It hurt like crazy. Tears rolled down my cheek.

The game ended with Cory's great shot. Through my watery eyes, I watched one of the tall men come striding toward us across the gym floor. He had a broad smile on his face.

What does he want? I wondered.

And then as he came closer, I squinted with my one good eye. And I recognized him.

"Oh, wow!" I cried. "I — I don't believe it!"

Franklin Howard. Yes. That was him, all right. Franklin Howard.

He had pulled off his cap, and I could see his shaved head. I recognized his smile. And the tattoo of a Chinese character on the side of his neck.

The Franklin Howard, center on our city's pro basketball team, the Stampede.

I should have known those three dudes were basketball players. Seven feet tall and hands as big as catchers' mitts? The other two stayed against the wall, jabbering with some kids.

Franklin Howard came charging up to Cory. He raised his fist, and he and Cory bumped knuckles. Cory's little hand looked like a pig's foot next to Howard's huge fist.

"Nice shot," Howard told Cory. "You totally faked this dude out." He pointed to me. "Sweet!"

Cory shrugged. "It was a lucky shot."

"No way," Howard insisted. "There's a big difference between luck and skill. And you've got skill, man. You've got skill — and you've got style."

"I . . . have a bug in my eye," I muttered. "That's why. . . ."

But the two of them weren't listening to me.

I rubbed the eye. *"Owwww."* The bug was stuck to my eyeball. It wouldn't budge.

"Would you like to come to a Stampede game?" Howard asked Cory. "I'd like you to come sit on the sidelines. You know. And hang with the team. Maybe you could pick up a few moves."

"Whoa," Cory replied. "That's awesome!"

He and Howard bumped knuckles again.

I rubbed my burning eye with the sleeve of my T-shirt. Tears rolled down my face.

"Oh, wow. That's totally sick!" Evan Kreel, one of my teammates, stared at the bug on my eye. "That's *huge*, dude. Like a spider."

"Let me see it, Lee," Coach Taylor said. He guided me to his office at the side of the gym.

"It — it's stuck," I stuttered. "It really hurts."

Taylor brought his face up to mine. "Yeah. It attached itself to the eyeball. Let me get a tweezer."

"Oh, wow." I really didn't want to have my eye tweezed. I squinted out into the gym. My teammates had all gathered around Franklin Howard.

Coach Taylor leaned over me, raising a metal tweezer in one hand. "Hold still," he said. He was gritting his teeth as he lowered the tweezer to my eye. "Man, that bug doesn't want to let go."

I held my breath. Finally, on the third try, he lifted the black thing off my eyeball. "Go rinse it with cold water," he told me.

I hurried to the locker room. I ran cold water over the eye. Then I stared into the mirror. The eye was bright red, but it felt a little better. I ran out into the gym.

At least, maybe I can get Franklin Howard's autograph, I thought.

That would be totally cool.

But Franklin and the other two players were gone.

"Hey, Lee — you missed it," Evan called. "Howard signed autographs for all of us."

Yeah, I missed it. Just my luck. Lucky Duck wins again.

14

I turned and started to slump back to the locker room. Coach Taylor came walking over. "Eye feel better?"

I nodded. "Yeah. Thanks a lot, Coach."

"No problem," he said. "Hey, listen. You'd better get your game up, Lee. I mean, if you want to win the scholarship. Cory wiped the floor with you today."

"Yeah. I guess," I muttered.

I stopped at the locker-room door and glanced back into the gym. Cory was showing off to the other players. He was spinning the basketball on one finger. They were clapping and cheering him on.

I sighed. Lucky Cory. *How will I ever beat him?*

4

Mom returned home from the high school a few minutes after I got home. Mom is tall and thin like me. She has straight blond hair that she usually ties behind her head in a ponytail. She wears glasses, but she hates them. She's always taking them off, then putting them back on.

She has been teaching Spanish at the high school for five years. She says someday maybe she'll graduate. My mom is the funny one in the family. Sometimes Dad has to tell her to be serious.

Arfy, our big, shaggy sheepdog, lumbered over to greet her. Arfy likes to jump on Mom and send her staggering back to the wall. He's very sweet. He just doesn't know he's as big as a bear.

Mom nuzzled Arfy for a while. Then she turned to me — and gasped. "Lee? Why is your eye red? Do you have pinkeye?"

"No. A bug flew into it," I said. "Coach Taylor had to tweeze it out."

"Ouch. How did your practice go?" she asked, kicking off her shoes.

"The usual," I said.

At dinner, Dad asked me about practice, too. Dad teaches Chemistry at the high school. Sometimes he wears his white lab coat around the house. He says he's just comfortable in it.

"Franklin Howard came to watch us play," I said.

"Nice!" Dad exclaimed. Dad is a big basketball fan. "Did he want to sign you up for the Stampede?"

"Not exactly," I said.

"Did you get his autograph?" Dad asked. He's a big autograph collector. He has all the presidents going back to Carter. He frames them and hangs them on the den wall.

I shook my head. "No. No autograph. But it was cool to see him."

I didn't say that everyone *else* got an autograph. I didn't want Dad to think I was a loser.

After dinner I was up in my room, in front of my laptop. I was visiting the website for the Summer Sports Camp for the eleven-millionth time.

The lake looked beautiful. They have an Olympic-sized pool, too. With a high-diving board. They have Olympic swimmers to give diving lessons.

And major league baseball players to give

17

batting and fielding lessons. And a Hall of Fame pitcher who will help you work on your fastball. Amazing, right?

If you're into basketball like me, they have that, too. They have experts to help you in every sport you might want to try. And you get to live in these awesome cabins with Wi-Fi and video games and big-screen TVs.

Heaven.

"I *have* to go there," I muttered at the screen. I gazed at the photo of the sparkling swimming pool. The pool was heated. Everyone got a one-hour free swim every day.

"I have to. *Have* to."

Sure, I had to worry about Laura winning the scholarship. She was a good athlete and captain of all the girls' teams.

But she wasn't my main problem.

My main problem, of course, was Lucky Duckworth.

"Maybe I can get lucky, too," I muttered. "Maybe . . ."

I heard a sound. I spun around to the door. Only Arfy.

The big dog stepped into my room. His head was down. He looked kind of droopy.

"Arfy, what are you doing in here?" I asked.

Arfy made a few loud coughing sounds. Like he was clearing his throat. He licked his snout furiously.

Then his stomach heaved. He opened his mouth wide and threw up on my carpet.

A big wave of lumpy yellow vomit poured out of his mouth. He made another groaning sound. And dropped another huge pile of vomit beside the first one.

I let out a long sigh.

Even my dog is bad luck!

How can I change my luck? Am I just DOOMED?

5

Mom came into my room while I was still cleaning up the vomit. She studied the carpet for a moment.

"You missed a spot," she said, pointing.

I rolled my eyes. "Thanks a lot, Mom."

She was holding a square brown package. "I forgot," she said. "This came in the mail for you."

I glanced up at it. "Who's it from?"

"Doesn't say," Mom said. The phone rang. She set the package down on my desk and hurried away to answer it.

I finished the cleanup. I washed my hands, but I couldn't get the smell off them.

I picked up the package. It was addressed to me with no return address. What could it be? I didn't remember sending for anything.

The package was very light. I shook it. Nothing rattled inside.

I tore off the brown paper and found a box underneath. In bright red letters, the top of the box read: INSTANT GOOD LUCK.

Huh? Had someone read my mind?

In smaller type, the box top said: *This rare good-luck charm never fails.*

I lifted the box and let the brown wrapping fall to the floor. "This has to be some kind of stupid joke," I muttered to Arfy.

The dog was watching me closely. He was hoping there would be food in the box.

Did Cory send this as a joke?

I shoved the box into my bottom desk drawer. I didn't even open it.

"Cory must think I'm a total moron," I said to Arfy. "Like I'm really going to believe in good-luck charms."

I slammed the desk drawer shut and forgot about it.

A few days later, six or seven kids gathered at the tennis court behind the school. They came for the first event in the Sports Camp competition.

A singles tennis match. Just one match against one opponent. The winners would score points for skill and style, awarded by Ms. Andersen, the school tennis coach.

Ms. Andersen is young and very pretty, with long, wavy brown hair and brown eyes and a great smile.

She doesn't dress like a teacher. She always wears T-shirts and jeans.

She matched up the players. Who did she match me up against? My pal Cory, of course.

Kids took out their rackets and began to take practice swings. We hit balls against the back wall of the school.

The court isn't in great shape. The surface is a little lumpy. Sometimes the ball takes crazy bounces. And the net is a little loose.

But it's the only court we have.

It was a sunny, warm day with a few low clouds drifting past. I did some warm-up exercises, swinging my arms from side to side. Loosening up.

I felt pretty good. Sometimes Cory and I play tennis on weekends, and we are about even. And maybe I beat him a few more times than he beats me.

Laura and a girl in our class named Shara Johnston were the first to play. We stopped our warm-ups to watch them.

Cory stepped up to me with a grin on his face, his dimple flashing. "Check it out," he said. He raised his racket in front of me.

"Is that new?" I asked.

He nodded. "My dad bought it for me. Look." He ran his fingers over the strings. "See? It's a new kind of racket. The string bed is suspended inside the frame."

I squinted at it. "What's that supposed to do?" I asked.

Cory's blue eyes sparkled in the sun. "It increases the sweet spot by eighty percent."

"The sweet spot?"

I knew what he was trying to do. He was trying to psych me out. He was trying to show me what a loser I was — before we even started to play.

"It cuts handle vibration by fifty percent," he added.

"Cool," I said. "Good luck with it, dude. I can still beat you." I twirled my racket in my hand.

He laughed and walked away. It wasn't a nice laugh.

Shara Johnston isn't a very good tennis player. She has no backhand at all. But Laura had a lot of trouble beating her.

Laura slumped off the court, drenched in sweat. She shook her head. "That was close. What a struggle," she said to me.

Cory popped up next to us. "You played really well — for a girl," he told Laura. He laughed.

"Shut up!" she said. She gave him a playful shove in the chest.

"Now watch Lee and me play," Cory told her. "Maybe you'll pick up some pointers." He turned and jogged onto the court, waving his fancy new racket in front of him.

"You mean like bad examples?" Laura called after him.

23

"Lee, get moving!" Ms. Andersen shouted. "Get this match going. Good luck!"

I'll need it, I thought. *If Cory has eighty percent more of a sweet spot, I'll need good luck.*

And as soon as I stepped onto the court, I knew I was in trouble.

My sore eye started to itch and throb. It still hadn't recovered from the bug that had to be tweezed from it. Tears rolled down my cheek.

It was hard to see clearly. Clouds floated over the sun. Long shadows spread over us.

I squinted hard with my one good eye. Cory has an awesome serve. My legs suddenly felt as if they weighed a hundred pounds each.

But I gritted my teeth and forced myself to move.

We play four-game sets. Two out of three sets wins the match.

I won the first set 4–2.

We changed court side. A lot of kids had gathered along the wire fence to watch us play. Laura flashed Cory a thumbs-up.

Why is she on his *side?* I wondered. *Just because he saved her life the other day? Just because he's blond and blue-eyed and lucky all the time, and everyone in school thinks he's awesome?*

Yeah. Maybe.

I forced myself to stop thinking about it. I tried to force all thoughts from my mind.

Tennis. Tennis. Tennis.

I repeated the word in my mind like a chant. It helped me concentrate.

I wiped the bad eye with the back of my hand. We started to play again. Even with only one good eye, I felt okay. I felt like I could finish him off.

That's when the sun came out. The clouds floated away. The sky brightened. The sun shone brightly again.

"Hey!" I shielded my eyes with one hand.

The sun was shining right in my eyes. One eye was totally blurred. The other eye was blinded by the sun. I couldn't see a thing.

Cory's serve bounced beside me and flew by.

I could see only a yellow-white glare. It was like someone kept flashing a camera right in my face.

I tried to shield my eyes and play at the same time. But that was impossible.

Cory sent another serve past me.

Not fair! I exclaimed to myself. *With the sun right in my eyes, he's going to KILL me.*

What am I going to do?

He killed me. Now we were even. We took a short break.

Ms. Andersen stepped up to the net. "Okay, guys," she called. "I don't want to make you tense or anything. But it's game-breaker time. This win counts big-time toward the scholarship. Good luck."

She didn't want to make us tense? Then why did she say that?

And did she have to keep saying "Good luck, good luck" all the time?

Cory and I touched rackets as we changed court side. I kept blinking, trying to force the white spots from my eyes. I mopped my runny eye with my T-shirt sleeve.

That sun was brutal. Sweat poured down my face. My hair was matted to my forehead.

I took a deep breath. I swung the racket from side to side. I wanted to make it feel like part of my arm.

I leaned forward and waited for Cory's serve.

And suddenly, I realized my luck had changed. I was about to win the tennis match.

Cory served. Too high. The ball bounced at least six inches past the line.

Cory couldn't see. He couldn't see a thing.

Because we had switched court sides. And now the sun was in *his* eyes!

Wow. I couldn't believe it. I felt like jumping up and down.

I watched him squinting and straining. The sun was like a big spotlight focused on his face.

He served again. Out!

Love–fifteen in favor of guess who? Me.

My heart pounded. This was too easy. Too easy! Sports Camp, here I come!

He served the next one. I hit it easily and bounced it right past him. Ha!

Love–thirty.

I won the first game easily. Three games to go to win the match.

Cory wiped sweat from his face. He shook his head angrily. His cheeks were red. He stared into the sun.

I tried not to laugh out loud. But I felt so good. It felt so good to be the lucky one for a change.

I tensed my muscles, preparing to serve.

That's when the shadows rolled over the court.

The sky darkened. Big clouds covered the sun.

Cory's whole body instantly relaxed. He was smiling now. He was loose. He was in the shade.

He won. He won everything. The sun stayed behind the clouds, and he won the match.

Lucky Duck won again.

As soon as the match was over, the sun came out again.

I pictured it grinning down on us. Like it had played a big joke on me.

Cory even controls the SUN! I thought.

"AAAAAAAAGH!" An angry cry burst from my throat.

I lost it. I totally lost it.

I just couldn't take all the good luck going Cory's way.

Without thinking, I swung my arm hard and let the tennis racket go sailing into the air.

Oh, no.

I saw what was about to happen.

Oh, no.

Nothing I could do. Too late. Too late. I couldn't stop it.

The racket flew into the back of Ms. Andersen's head.

CLONNNNK. It sounded like wood crashing into a wall as it smashed against her skull.

She uttered a high scream — and dropped to the ground.

Kids along the side of the tennis court gasped and cried out. Then everyone went silent.

I couldn't move. I couldn't breathe.

Did I really do that?

Okay. I threw the tennis racket. But could I really be unlucky enough to bean Ms. Andersen in the head with it? And knock her out cold?

Everyone hurried over to her. They formed a silent circle.

Cory and Laura leaned over her. I stayed at the back of the circle, afraid to look.

Forget Sports Camp, I told myself. *You're going to prison for this, Lee.*

Ms. Andersen groaned. She sat up and rubbed the back of her head. She blinked several times. Then she smoothed her dark hair.

"I'm okay," she said. "I guess I was mostly startled."

She's not dead!

Huddled behind some kids, I let out a long sigh of relief.

Cory helped Ms. Andersen to her feet. She brushed off her jeans. Then she rubbed the back of her head again.

She gazed around the circle of kids till she spotted me. "Uh . . . Lee, could you come over here?" she asked.

Uh-oh. Doom time.

I took a few trembling steps toward her. "I — I'm sorry," I stammered.

She frowned at me. "Lee, you're going to have to work on your sportsmanship, aren't you?" she said. "You know, sportsmanship is important in this contest."

"It . . . was an accident," I said. "The racket . . . it slipped from my hand."

Lame. I know.

"I know it was an accident," Ms. Andersen said in a soft voice. "But you were upset about losing the match, right? And you lost your temper."

I nodded. "Well . . . yes. But I didn't mean —"

She raised a hand to silence me. The sunlight flashed in her brown eyes. "Cory and Laura have a good head start toward the scholarship," she said. "I want to see you try harder, Lee. And I don't want to see you lose your temper again."

31

"Yes. Right. I mean, no problem," I stammered. "I'm really sorry. I mean, really."

Yes. I was sorry I threw my racket. Sorry I smashed her in the head. Sorry I lost the match. Sorry I had such bad luck.

I trudged home with my head down. I felt so sorry for myself, I didn't look at the corner and almost got run over by a bunch of teenagers on bikes. They shouted all kinds of names at me.

I deserved it.

What a bad start for winning that scholarship. "Lee, you're going to need a lot of help if you're going to win now." That's what I told myself.

And I guess that's what made me think of that package. The box with the good-luck charm that I'd stuffed into a desk drawer.

Maybe I should give it a try, I decided. *After all, I'm totally desperate.*

It couldn't hurt — right?

Arfy greeted me at the front door. He leaped onto my chest and knocked me back against the wall. Then he pinned me there with his huge front paws and licked most of the skin off my face.

"Good dog. Good dog. I'm happy to see you, too!" I cried. I had to wrestle him to the floor to escape his greeting.

I was eager to get past him. I wanted to check out that good-luck charm. I needed it to start working — fast!

I took the stairs two at a time and lurched into

my bedroom. Arfy came clumping up the stairs, close behind me. He kept bumping the back of my legs, and I nearly tripped.

Into my room. I dove to my desk. I bent down and tugged open the bottom drawer.

I shoved some papers and things out of the way. Then I pulled up the box with the red letters.

INSTANT GOOD LUCK.

I read those words a couple of times. I felt excited. Maybe I was holding something that really did work. Something that would give me the luck I needed to defeat Lucky Duckworth.

I read the tiny type. *This rare good-luck charm never fails.*

"What could it be?" I said to Arfy. He had his furry head raised and was sniffing at the box. "Think it's just a rabbit's foot?"

I tore off the top of the box. The item inside was wrapped in a ball of red tissue paper.

Carefully, I unwrapped the tissue paper — and gazed wide eyed at the thing inside.

"Ohhh, sick," I moaned. "It's . . . disgusting."

I stared at the ugly thing in my hand. It was hard and kind of crusty. At first, I thought it was covered with black hair. Then I realized it was scraggly feathers.

Some kind of horrible, dried-up claw. Was it a bird claw?

I turned the box on its side and read the words: RARE VULTURE CLAW.

Vulture claw?

It sure didn't look like a good-luck charm. I turned it over in my hand. It had three bony talons. The cracked nails at the ends were yellow and curled.

It looked like something out of a horror movie!

I held it up and scraped the air with it. *"Caw caw cawwww."* I made an ugly bird sound.

Arfy barked. He kept his eyes on it. I could tell he didn't like it.

I tried to picture the bird that lost this claw. A scrawny black vulture. I pictured it hopping on one claw.

Didn't vultures swoop down and eat dead things on the ground?

Since when were vultures *good* luck?

The claw was attached to a slender black rope. Like a pendant. I swung it in my hand. I couldn't decide whether to wear the claw or not.

Arfy barked again.

"I know, boy," I said. "It's kind of gross. But I need all the help I can get."

"Lee." Mom stepped into the room.

I slid the claw into the desk drawer and closed it. I didn't want her asking questions.

"What is it, Mom?"

She handed me a white envelope. It had a small orange and yellow pizza on one corner. "This just came for you," she said. She turned and headed back downstairs.

I tore it open and read the letter inside.

The letter was from Pizza Planet. My favorite pizza place.

"Whoa . . . whoa . . ." I muttered to myself as my eyes ran down the page.

"Hey, Arfy — it says I won!" I cried.

The letter said I won a drawing. My contest card was picked. I won a free pizza dinner for me and my whole family!

"Wow!" I cried, jumping to my feet. I pumped both fists in the air. I'd never won *anything* before! Never.

I read the letter again. I was excited. Free pizza!

I pulled out the ugly vulture claw. Was it possible? Had the good luck started already?

I grabbed the slender rope and slid it down over my head. I straightened the claw over the front of my T-shirt.

A minute ago, I didn't believe in good-luck charms. But now I *believed.*

I'm going to wear this thing forever! I decided.

Arfy barked again. Then he jumped. He snapped at the claw. He was trying to pull it away from me.

"No, Arfy!" I screamed.

I pushed the big dog away with one hand. With the other hand, I tucked the claw out of sight under my T-shirt.

My elbow bumped the box. A small square of paper fluttered out from inside it.

Before it hit the floor, Arfy grabbed it in his mouth. He turned and ran off with it, like it was some kind of prize.

I laughed. He looked so funny. Like a criminal eager to check out his loot.

I read the pizza letter again and let out a cheer. I felt great.

I rubbed the claw under my T-shirt. I had a feeling my life was going to change now. I had a feeling *everything* was going to change.

And guess what?

Everything did!

10

Mom and Dad were excited about the free dinner at Pizza Planet, too. They said maybe we'd go Friday night.

I didn't tell them about the vulture claw. They don't believe in good-luck charms. Dad is a science teacher, remember. He only believes in science.

I knew they'd only laugh at me about wearing the claw. That's why I kept it private. I could feel it against my chest as I sat down for dinner. It felt a little scratchy, but I didn't care.

Arfy squeezed past my legs and sat down under the table. That's where he goes every time we eat. One night a long time ago, a hot dog fell off the table, and Arfy caught it. Now he waits every night for something else to fall.

"What's for dinner?" I asked.

"I made those spicy Buffalo chicken wings you like," Mom said. "And mashed potatoes."

"My favorite!" I cried.

More good luck. This claw was *amazing*.

Dinner was awesome. Best Buffalo chicken wings ever.

"How was the tennis match?" Dad asked. He was wearing his white lab coat. He wasn't going to be happy when he saw the orange chicken stain on the sleeve.

"Not great," I told him. "The sun got in my eyes, and Cory beat me."

"Bad luck," Dad said, shaking his head.

"That's no problem," I said. "I'm going to ask for a rematch. I know I'll whip his butt next time."

Mom frowned at me. "Language," she said. "That's not how we talk at the dinner table."

"Sorry," I muttered. I was feeling so good, I couldn't help myself. I wanted to dance around the room screaming my head off.

I mean, I waited a *long time* to have a little good luck.

And guess what? The good luck kept on coming.

Dad said he had a present for me.

And what was it? *Battle Warrior World 2* for my Nintendo DS. The game I'd been begging him to buy me for months!

I stared at it wide eyed. My heart was thumping like crazy.

More good luck. More.

I couldn't wait. I shoved the game into my DS and started to blast away with both thumbs.

"Yes! Yes! Awesome!"

I beat the first level in less than two minutes!

Mom and Dad were still eating. Mom made a face at Dad. "I don't approve of war games."

Dad shrugged. He squinted at me. "Lee, you didn't read the instructions. How come you never stop to read the instructions for anything?"

"Don't need them," I muttered.

POW POW BLAMMMMBLAMBLAMMMM.

"Instructions are for babies," I said. "Look. I'm already on level two. This game is awesome!"

Dinner was over. Mom said I could go up to my room. I didn't have to help clean up tonight.

More good luck!

I ran up to my room and shut the door. I remembered something. My grades.

Miss Harrison, my science teacher, said our grades might be posted online today.

I let out a sigh. I knew this wasn't going to be my best report card. I'd messed up on two math tests. Just bad luck. I studied the wrong pages.

And I handed in a history paper two days late. I don't know why. I'd been carrying it around in my backpack. And I just forgot to hand it in.

So . . . I wasn't expecting the best grades in Lee Hargrove history. Maybe . . . maybe I could slide by with all B's this semester.

I sat down in front of my laptop and brought up the class website. Then I typed in my password — A-R-F-Y.

Were our grades posted? Yes.

I leaned forward and stared at my report card on the screen.

"I . . . don't . . . believe . . . it," I muttered.

All A's.

I tugged the claw out from under my shirt. I squeezed it gently.

"Thank you!" I whispered. "Thank you!"

I tucked the claw back. "I'm never taking you off," I told it. "I'm never giving up all this good luck. Good luck is *fun!*"

Did my good luck last forever?

Three guesses.

11

In school the next morning, my luck continued. Miss Harrison called me over before class.

She glanced through some papers. Then she smiled at me. "Lee, you're way ahead of the class on this science unit," she said. "You don't need to take the test today."

"I — I don't?" I stammered. Was I hearing her correctly? Skip a test?

"Why don't you go to the library and do some research online?" Miss Harrison said.

"Yeah. Sure. No problem," I said. "Thanks." I practically skipped out of the classroom.

The claw bumped my chest as I strode down the hall. It felt good.

My lucky vulture claw. It was bringing me good luck every minute.

I felt awesome. My whole life had changed. I was a brand-new Lee. And I liked it.

At lunchtime, Laura Grodin actually smiled at me. That didn't happen very often.

42

"Hey, wait up, Lee," she called. She trotted across the crowded hall.

The claw had come out from under my T-shirt. It dangled in front of me.

Laura squinted at it. "Yuck. What's that? An animal claw? Is it real?"

"I think it's a fake," I lied. "I . . . just thought it was cool. Found it at a garage sale."

I didn't like lying to Laura. But I didn't want to tell her the truth. No way I wanted to tell her it was a real vulture claw that instantly brought all kinds of good luck.

What if she went and bought one? That wouldn't be good.

Laura rubbed her finger on the crusty black feathers. "Ugh. Gross." She made a disgusted face. Then she saw some friends across the hall and ran off to talk to them.

I hid the claw under my shirt and headed to the lunchroom. I had a smile on my face. That was the first time Laura ever paid any attention to me. Thanks to the claw.

I turned the corner. I was nearly to the lunchroom when I spotted a small blue object on the floor. It was half-hidden under a locker.

I bent down and picked it up. A wallet. A fat wallet stuffed with money and cards.

"Lee?" I heard a woman's voice behind me. "Did you find it?"

I spun around to see Ms. Lincoln, our principal,

hurrying across the hall toward me. She had her eyes on the wallet in my hand.

"Did you find my wallet?" she repeated.

I handed it to her.

"Oh, thank goodness!" she cried. "I've been searching for hours. Thank you, Lee. Thank you!"

"It . . . was under the locker," I said. I pointed. "A lucky find."

"It sure was!" she exclaimed. She reached into the wallet and pulled out a ten-dollar bill. "A little reward for you," she said. She stuffed the money into my hand.

"No. I can't —" I started to give it back to her.

But she closed my fist around it. "Keep it," she said. "You deserve a reward. You saved my life."

She turned and hurried back toward her office. I gazed at the ten-dollar bill in my hand. *How lucky was that?*

I tucked it into my jeans and stepped into the crowded, noisy lunchroom. I wasn't interested in lunch. I was too excited to be hungry.

I knew what I had to do. I marched up to Cory. He was sitting at the front table with a bunch of kids from our class.

"Yo, Lee. What's up?" he said. He had a mouthful of peanut butter and jelly. That's what he eats for lunch every day. He says it's his lucky sandwich.

But I knew who had the luck today. He could eat ten jars of peanut butter and jelly. Things had changed.

"I want a rematch," I said. "I want to have a do-over of our tennis match."

He grinned at me. He was so sure of himself, he didn't hesitate for a second.

"No problem," he said. "A rematch. Let's do it."

I rubbed the claw under my shirt. No way I could lose this time.

No way.

12

Cory and I insisted on a new match. Ms. Andersen didn't really understand. But she said if we wanted it so badly, we could do it.

Word got around school, and a lot of kids showed up to watch.

Some kids called it a "grudge match." I think that's why a lot of them came.

Also, word had gone around school that I'd tossed my racket and knocked Ms. Andersen to the ground. I think some kids were waiting for me to lose it again.

But I didn't lose it. This time, I won.

This time, the sun hid behind clouds when I was facing it. And when we switched court sides, it shone brightly again and blinded Cory.

So I won two sets to none.

Good luck. Either you have it or you don't.

I was so happy, I let out a shout of victory and leaped over the net. Cory just stood there shaking his head. I could tell by the upset look on his face that I had him worried.

I knew I could win the Sports Camp scholarship easily. With the help of the vulture claw, of course.

I laughed and tried to joke with Cory. But he didn't want to talk. He turned and stomped away, angrily slapping his fancy new tennis racket against his hand.

I saw Laura flash me a warm smile from the side of the court. She gave me a double thumbs-up.

Too bad, Laura, I thought. *You and Cory don't stand a chance now.*

I pulled out the ugly black claw and kissed it. Then I tucked it back under my shirt.

I hummed to myself all the way home. I felt like dancing. Or skipping.

I let myself in and tossed my tennis racket case and backpack to the floor. I heard heavy footsteps in the hall. Arfy barked and came running to greet me.

"Hey — down boy. Down!"

Why did I say that? He never listens to me. Arfy's so big that he doesn't obey a single command. He knows he can do whatever he feels like.

"Arfy — please!"

He leaped on me, pressing his big paws on my shoulders. I stumbled back against the wall.

"Stop!" I cried. He was frantically licking my face. My cheeks dripped with thick slobber. "Stop it!"

I tried to push him off. He pawed at my T-shirt collar.

"Hey!" I let out a cry as he grabbed the vulture claw in his teeth. With a hard tug, he snatched it off the rope.

"NO!" I screamed.

Arfy clamped the claw in his teeth. Then he pushed off from my chest with both paws. He spun around and galloped out of the room.

"No! Arfy — come back!" I wailed. "It isn't a dog toy! Oh, nooooo. Come back with that!"

13

I chased him down the back hall. He ran into my parents' room and tried to jump on their bed.

But I tackled him around his middle and wrestled him to the floor. I made a grab for the vulture claw, and it slid easily out from between his teeth.

He snapped at it. But I swung it out of his reach and rolled away from him. "Not a toy!" I shouted. "Not a toy."

Arfy made a whimpering sound. He stared up at the claw.

I studied it carefully. It was dripping with saliva. One of the talons was torn — just a little bit. Not too bad.

"Bad dog," I scolded Arfy. But he was already trotting out of the room, his tail wagging. Dogs have very short attention spans.

I tried to dry off the claw on the front of my shirt. Then I slid it back in place.

"Close call," I muttered.

Arfy almost ruined my good luck. Of course, he didn't know what he was doing. He was just being a dog.

But I needed this good-luck charm. *Needed* it. Like breathing.

I let out a sigh of relief. The claw felt good against my chest. I vowed I'd keep it snug and safe from now on.

I started up the stairs to my room. I was nearly at the top when my shoe caught on something. A lump in the carpet?

"Owwwww!" I let out a scream as I lost my balance. I fell hard onto my side — hit my head — and bounced all the way down.

Bump bump bump bump.

I landed at the bottom. The surprise took my breath away. My heart was racing. Pain rolled up and down my body.

I didn't move till I could breathe normally. Then I sat up with a groan. The back of my neck ached. My left ankle throbbed. I tested it. It wasn't broken, but it sure hurt.

"Oh, wow," I muttered. "Wow." I shook my head, trying to shake away the dizziness and pain. Groaning, I climbed to my feet.

"That's not supposed to happen," I said to myself. "I'm supposed to have all good luck."

Then I thought, *Well, I didn't break my neck.*

I could have broken my ankle or my arm. I guess the claw kept me from seriously hurting myself.

I pulled it out from under my shirt. I turned it over in my hand. The fall didn't crush it or anything.

I kissed it and tucked it back in. Then I started back up the stairs.

This time, I gripped the banister as I climbed. My ankle still throbbed, but I could stand on it.

I stepped into my room. One of my baseball posters had fallen off the wall. It was lying upside down on the floor.

I rolled it up and leaned it against the wall. *I'll tape it back up later*, I decided.

I sat down at my desk and opened the laptop. I powered it on and waited for the screen to light up.

Miss Harrison puts her homework assignments online every afternoon. I went to our school site to see what work I had to do.

The page started to come up. But then the screen suddenly went black.

I heard a sizzling sound. Like bacon frying on the stove.

"What's up with that?" I muttered.

And then I jumped to my feet as black smoke poured up from my laptop.

I knocked the desk chair over as I staggered back two or three steps.

And then I gasped as bright orange and yellow flames flickered over the keyboard.

My laptop! It was on fire!

14

I stared in horror as the flames danced over the keyboard. My panic lasted only a few seconds.

I dove forward and slammed the lid shut. Would that put out the flames?

Black smoke sizzled up from the back. Then the smoke faded away.

Silence.

I didn't move. I froze there, holding my breath, waiting to see if the flames would shoot up again.

Finally, I touched the lid. It wasn't hot. I flipped it open.

The flames were gone. The keyboard was charred black. A lot of the keys had melted onto one another.

Ruined. It was totally destroyed.

How did that happen? I just powered it on, and it burst into flames.

I knew my parents would take it back to the store and buy me a new one. But all my work was lost. My history notes were on it. And my book report that was due next Friday. And science stuff . . .

My birthday party photos. The photos I snapped on the class trip . . .

All lost.

I stared down at the black, melted keys. *What bad luck.*

I felt the vulture claw press against my chest. I pulled it out and studied it. It seemed okay except for the little tear on one talon.

"What's wrong with you?" I asked it. "Where is the good luck? You've got to come through for me now."

That night, I couldn't sleep.

I felt jumpy. I couldn't lie still. I forced my eyes shut and tried counting down from one thousand.

But I couldn't concentrate. I turned onto my side. Then I tried the other side.

I felt like a restless animal in a zoo. The kind that prowls its cage, back and forth, poking its snout through the spaces between the cage bars.

I sat up and rested my head against the headboard. The bedroom window was open, and white moonlight poured in. Silvery white moonlight almost as bright as day.

I shut my eyes, but I couldn't force out the light.

I knew I was sleepy. My eyelids were heavy. I *had* to sleep. But my brain was spinning. And the bright white light . . . the light was calling me . . . forcing me to my feet.

I stood up. I paced my room, my bare feet cold against the carpet. I have a long, narrow room. Not much room to pace.

Like a caged animal, I thought again.

I spotted my guitar propped against the closet door. I lifted it up and carried it to the bed. I propped it in my lap.

Playing the guitar always relaxes me.

I balanced it on my lap. Then I started to strum.

Something was wrong. It didn't sound right. It didn't . . . *feel* right.

I squinted into the moonlight. I raised my hand.

And opened my mouth in a scream of horror.

My hand! Where was it? What *happened* to my hand?

I gaped in disbelief at the ragged talons and thick feathers. My hand had turned into a CLAW!

15

My talons curled around the guitar neck. The strings all started to pop.

Pop pop poppop POP.

The final *pop* was loud enough to wake me up. "Huh?"

I stared at the ceiling. Shadows shifted above my head in a pale square of moonlight.

I'm lying in bed, I realized.

I was asleep.

It was a dream. Yes?

I raised both hands from under the covers. Yes. I had two hands. No giant bird claw.

A nightmare. But it seemed so real. I could still see every detail.

Still see the big feathery claw at the end of my arm wrapping around the guitar neck.

I *never* have nightmares. I mean, really never. Not since I was a little kid.

Usually, I can't remember my dreams at all.

But mostly, my dreams are about kids at school, and my parents, and playing sports. Boring stuff.

Never nightmares. Never horrifying dreams that wake me up screaming.

Or was I only screaming in the dream?

I checked out my hands again. Just to make sure.

They were fine. Perfectly normal hands.

My heart was still beating hard. A shiver rolled down my body. It was warm in my room, especially under the covers. Why was I shivering?

I pulled up the vulture claw to examine it.

Yes, I wore it when I slept. I wasn't taking chances. I wanted good luck twenty-four hours a day.

The light from outside was dim. I raised the claw close to my face and squinted hard at it.

I gasped when the three talons moved.

It can't be alive. It CAN'T be!

"It's just the darkness," I murmured to myself. "That nightmare — it upset me. I'm *seeing* things."

But to my horror, the claw leaped from my hand. It snapped forward — and grabbed me by the throat.

"*Unnnnh.*" I made a choking sound as the talons gripped my skin. They tightened. Wrapped around the skin under my chin.

Choked me.

"*Unnnnh.*"

Tighter. Tighter. The claw squeezed so hard, I wanted to scream in pain.

But I couldn't scream. I couldn't breathe.

The claw gripped my windpipe.

"*Unh unnnnh.*" I couldn't make a sound.

I struggled to pull it off with both hands.

It was too strong. Clamped on too tightly. I couldn't budge it.

Oh, nooooo.

I knew what was happening.

It was going to KILL me.

16

"Lee? Are you okay?"

"Lee — what's your problem?"

I opened my eyes to see Mom and Dad rushing into my bedroom.

Dad clicked on the ceiling light. He was in his striped pajama bottoms. Mom was tying the belt on her blue bathrobe. Her hair fell in tangles over her face.

The bright light made me blink. It took a few seconds for everything to come into focus.

I realized I was sitting on the edge of my bed. My pajamas were all twisted. My face prickled with cold sweat.

Glancing down, I saw that I was holding the claw tightly in front of me.

"What was that scream?" Dad asked, leaning over me. "Did something frighten you?"

"I — I —" I cleared my throat. I raised the claw up to him. "It grabbed me," I said. "It was . . . choking me."

Mom uttered a short cry. She brushed her hair off her face with both hands. Her eyes were on the vulture claw. "Lee, what *is* that thing?"

"It's . . . something I got in the mail," I said.

Dad ran a finger over my throat. He squinted at me. Turned my head gently from side to side.

"You had a nightmare," he said softly.

"Yes. A nightmare," Mom repeated. She shivered. "That ugly thing would give *me* nightmares, too!"

"Dad, n-no," I stammered. "It wasn't a nightmare. It was real. It grabbed my neck and —"

"No." Dad raised a hand, motioning for me to stop. "There aren't any marks on your neck, Lee. No pinch marks. No scratches. Nothing."

"It was a dream," Mom said, coming up beside him. "Weird," she added. "You never have nightmares."

I blinked. I gazed down at the claw. It wasn't moving. It was stiff and still.

What just happened to me? I wondered.

Was it a nightmare inside a nightmare?

In the first nightmare, I had a claw instead of a hand. Maybe I never woke up from that dream. Maybe I slid right into the next dream.

And dreamed that the claw snapped over my windpipe.

That had to be what happened. A dream inside a dream. One frightening nightmare after another.

I settled back under the covers. Dad pulled the blanket under my chin.

"Maybe you should put that ugly claw away, Lee," he said.

"Yes. If it's giving you bad dreams, throw it away," Mom said.

"No way," I replied. I tucked the claw under the blanket. "It's a good-luck charm. It brought me a lot of good luck."

"Good luck? It doesn't look like a good-luck charm to *me*!" Mom said, shaking her head. She led Dad out the door. They clicked off the light.

I lay there on my back in the darkness. I could feel the claw resting lightly on my chest.

Thumpthump thump thumpthump.

That heavy thumping was my heart, right? It wasn't the claw thumping against my chest. Right?

Right?

17

The next morning, it was hard to wake up. Dad is my alarm clock. He shouts, "Wake up! Rise and shine!" into my room every morning at seven.

It usually takes only one shout. But this morning, he had to give the alarm three times.

Groaning, I sat up. It took all my strength to climb out from under the covers. I still felt shaken from those nightmares. They were just too real.

I checked my hands. Normal. Not claws.

I yawned and stretched. I could smell bacon frying downstairs. It was Friday. Bacon and scrambled eggs day.

Mom believes in a big breakfast. She says it gets you going for the day.

I needed to wake up and get going strong. This afternoon was the next competition for the scholarship. The bowling tournament.

I squeezed the claw under my pajama shirt. I needed all the luck I could get. Bowling is not my best sport.

I took a hot shower. Then I went to the closet to pick out some clothes.

I pulled my best jeans from the top shelf. And my favorite T-shirt — the red one with a big black thumbs-up on the front. I started to pull on the jeans — then stopped. I squinted at the front. What was the dark stain on the front? A big dark circle around the zipper.

It made it look like I had wet myself!

Oh, well. No way I could wear these jeans to school. I heaved them to the floor and went back to my closet for another pair.

Then I raised the T-shirt over my head and started to pull it on. Oh, wait. I couldn't believe it. Both sleeves had big rips at the armpits. The shirt was totally torn.

Mom would never let me wear it to school. I sighed. My favorite T-shirt — ruined. I tossed it on top of the stained jeans and went to choose another one.

What was up with my clothes? How did they get messed up just sitting in my closet?

I went into the bathroom to brush my hair. It's thick and wiry, and I can't really get it to stay flat or anything. But today, I heard a snap. And the comb broke in half.

"Huh?" I stared at the two pieces in my hand. This day was *not* off to a great start.

The claw bounced against my chest as I hurried down the stairs to breakfast. Mom was dressed for school. She stood at the stove, poking the bacon. Out the window, I saw Dad watering his tomato plants.

Mom turned. "No more nightmares?"

I shook my head. "No. I slept fine. But my good jeans? The new ones? They have a stain —"

Mom pointed to the fridge. "Pull out six eggs," she said. "Two for each of us."

She never really hears me in the morning. Too much on her mind. I decided I'd tell her about the jeans and T-shirt later.

I pulled open the door to the fridge. The eggs were on the top shelf of the door. I reached for two eggs — then stopped.

Whoa.

I heard a cracking sound. The sound repeated all down the row of eggs.

Crack craaack craaackcraack.

I let out a cry as the eggs cracked open — and scrawny, wet claws came poking out. A dozen sticky claws clenching and unclenching their bony talons.

18

"Noooooooo!"

A long moan escaped my throat.

"What's wrong?" Mom cried. She dropped her spatula and came running over to the fridge. "Lee, what's all the screaming about?"

"I — I —" I pointed to the two rows of eggs in the door. Then I blinked. I squinted hard.

The eggs were perfectly okay. No cracks. No claws poking out from inside the shells.

"Oh, wow," I muttered.

Mom put a hand on my shoulder. "What's wrong?"

"I think . . . I'm seeing things," I said.

She led me to the kitchen table. I dropped into my chair, my brain buzzing. She carried the eggs from the fridge and started to scramble them.

Dad waved to me from outside. I stared out the window at him, but I didn't wave back.

I'm totally messed up, I told myself.

I was seeing things. *Hallucinating* is the word for it. First I had nightmares about claws. And now I was seeing claws when I was awake!

My clothes were ruined. My comb cracked in half.

Bad luck. Bad luck and nightmares and hallucinations . . .

I had a sick feeling. Like a heavy rock weighing down my stomach.

Has the good luck from the vulture claw run out?

Has the claw turned against me?

I knew it worked before. I knew it could change my life. Was there anything I could do to bring back the good luck?

19

After school, Coach Taylor drove six of us to the bowling alley in his SUV. Laura, Cory, and the other kids laughed and goofed on one another the whole way. I sat in a corner in the backseat and stayed pretty quiet.

I felt tense all day. My hands shook. My heart raced.

I kept expecting to see more claws pop out at me. I kept expecting to be the star of a horror movie that only I could see.

Now I felt even more stressed. I knew I had to win the bowling match to stay in the race for the scholarship. And Laura and Cory were both better bowlers than me.

Come on, claw, I repeated to myself. *Do your thing. Please work for me.*

"Hey, Lee, what's up?" Cory turned around in his seat and grinned at me. "Why are you so quiet?"

"Just thinking," I muttered.

"Thinking about how I can beat you left-handed?" Cory said.

I groaned. "Cory — you *are* left-handed. Remember?"

He laughed. "Oh, yeah. Right."

Laura slapped Cory's shoulder. "Shut up, Cory. You don't have to brag all the time."

"I know I don't have to brag," Cory said. "I can beat him without bragging. I can beat you, too, Laura."

"Shut up," Laura repeated. It was one of her favorite phrases. Sometimes she *started* a conversation with it.

"Tell you what," Cory said, his dimple flashing. "Maybe you two can come visit me at Sports Camp this summer."

"Ha-ha. You're so funny," Laura said. She gave him a shove.

I stayed out of it. I just wanted to focus. Focus on doing my best. Focus on winning today.

Coach Taylor pulled the SUV into the parking lot. The place was called Roll-a-Bowl Lanes. It was a long, low building with painted bowling balls bouncing across the front. A neon sign read: Burgers! Fries! Best Bowling for Miles! We followed the coach inside. I counted about twenty bowling lanes. Only a few were being used. Not too many people bowl at four o'clock on a Friday afternoon.

I saw an ice-cream counter across from where you get your bowling shoes. And a small burger place with four or five tables next door to it.

The manager gave us lanes at the very end. We trotted down to them and picked out our bowling balls. I had to have a blue one. That's my favorite color.

I sat down on the bench next to Laura and a sixth grader named Gray Haddox. Gray is a big dude with short blond hair and a red face that always looks like he's blushing. He lives for sports. He's on the soccer team and the track team. Actually, I think he's on *every* team!

I don't know Gray very well. He's very shy and quiet — except when he's playing sports. And he hangs out with another crowd, some kids from the high school.

Gray bowled a strike on his first turn. He pumped his big fist in the air and came back to the bench with a huge smile on his red face.

Laura and Cory got off to bad starts. Laura's first two rolls were gutter balls. She scored a big zip.

Cory knocked down only three pins in two tries. He muttered angrily to himself, slapping the ball. Like it was the ball's fault.

I kissed the claw. Then stepped up for my first try. I'm not a great bowler. I can never decide which foot to lead with.

But I got off to a good start. I bowled an eight in the first frame. I had a spare in the second frame. And an eight in the third frame.

By the tenth frame, Cory, Laura, and Gray were ahead of me. But only by a few points. The other kids were way behind us.

I studied the score sheet. If I could bowl a spare in this frame, I would win the game.

Now I was really excited. *I can do it*, I told myself. *I can win this thing.*

My heart began to race. My hands were sweaty. I dried them off on a towel.

I stepped onto the lane. I took a deep breath. Raised the ball . . . Sent it rolling down the center of the alley . . .

. . . And knocked down eight pins.

Okay. The remaining two pins were close together on the right. An easy spare.

An easy spare to make me the winner.

I waited for the ball to return. I wiped my sweaty hands on the towel again.

I took another deep breath. Then I stepped onto the lane.

I could see Cory, Laura, and Gray watching me. Intense stares on their faces.

I touched the claw under my shirt.

Please — come through for me. Please — bring me good luck.

Would the claw do its job?

I pulled the ball back and started my approach.

20

I took two steps. Swung my arm forward . . .

. . . And the ball slipped off my hand.

It dropped hard and fast.

I heard a heavy thud as it crushed the top of my bowling shoe.

"*Owwwwwww!*" I opened my mouth in a howl.

A crushing pain shot up my leg.

I dropped to the floor, twisting in agony.

"My toes! I broke my toes! I broke my foot!" I shrieked.

Gray dropped down beside me. He put a hand on my shoulder and kept telling me to calm down. Help was on the way.

By the time Coach Taylor showed up, I'd stopped screaming and writhing on the floor. But my foot still throbbed with pain.

The coach and Gray lifted me to my feet and helped me to the bench. Taylor gently pulled the bowling shoe and the sock off my foot. He tested the ankle and the toes.

"The foot isn't broken," he said. He massaged the foot carefully. He frowned. "Maybe you broke your little toe. But there's nothing you can do for that."

I swallowed. "You mean — ?"

"You just have to put up with the pain," Taylor said. "It'll feel better after a while."

I rolled my eyes. "After a while?"

The whole foot throbbed. I couldn't believe every bone wasn't broken.

I slumped onto the bench. I had lost the game.

Laura won by three points. Cory was one point behind her. Gray came in third.

Coach Taylor was studying the score sheet. "Do I get any points for sportsmanship? Or for improvement?" I called to him.

He didn't answer.

A cold feeling of dread rolled over me. In the competition for the scholarship, I was definitely falling further and further behind.

We changed back into our real shoes. My foot didn't hurt that much. But the little toe was so painful, I couldn't touch it.

It was bright red and totally swollen. I squeezed the foot into my shoe, and I limped after Cory and Laura toward the exit.

We were nearly to the door when Cory bent down and picked something up from under a chair. "Hey, check it out," he said. He held it up to us. "I found a cell phone."

We followed him to the front desk. He handed the phone to the manager. "Someone dropped their phone," Cory said.

The manager was a huge, bald guy in a sleeveless red T-shirt. The shirt only came down halfway over his belly. A red and blue tattoo of a bowling ball rippled on his right bicep.

He grinned at Cory. He had a gold tooth right in the middle of his mouth. "That's so nice of you to return it," he said. "Most people would just walk away with it."

He pointed across the room. "Dude, go over to the ice-cream booth," he told Cory. "Have a free sundae — on me."

"Hey, thanks," Cory said. He gave the manager a funny two-fingered salute.

We followed Cory to the ice-cream booth. He got a huge hot fudge sundae — for free. Laura and I had to pay for our ice-cream cones.

Cory flashed me a thumbs-up. "Excellent sundae," he said. "Guess my luck is still good."

I forced a smile. But I wasn't smiling inside.

My little toe was *killing* me. It throbbed and ached so bad, it was hard to *think*.

Yes, Cory's luck was still good. And what was mine?

Bad bad bad.

Nothing but bad.

I stared at Cory gulping down a big spoon of ice cream covered in hot fudge. And as I watched him, the ice cream fell out of my cone and landed with a *splat* on top of my shoe.

I didn't even bother to wipe it off.

My heart started to pound. I realized my life was spinning out of control.

I was losing the competition. Hallucinating. Getting injured.

At least it can't get any worse than this, I thought.

Boy, was I wrong.

21

At home, I hurried upstairs to my room. My foot felt better now. Or maybe I was getting used to the pain. But each step on the broken toe reminded me about my bad luck.

I knew I had to change my luck — right away. I didn't want to get hurt again. I didn't want to see claws everywhere I looked.

I knew what I had to do.

I had to get rid of the vulture claw.

I grabbed the rope pendant and tugged it off my neck. I held it up and studied the ugly thing.

It had changed from good luck to bad. And I just realized why.

I tugged at the torn talon. Arfy did this. It was all that big dumb dog's fault.

He took it from me and chewed on it. He got dog saliva all over it. That's when it changed. Arfy ruined it.

I wrapped the rope around it and stuffed the claw into my T-shirt drawer. I pushed it down under all the T-shirts. I didn't want to see it again. I didn't want to think about it.

I'll make my own good luck from now on.

That's what I was thinking when Mom stepped into my room. She was carrying a stack of neatly folded socks and underwear. "These are clean," she said. "You can put them away."

"No problem," I said.

She dumped them on my bed. "How was the bowling thing?" she said.

"Don't ask," I replied.

"That bad?"

"Worse," I said. "I dropped the ball on my foot."

She squinted at me. "You're supposed to throw it, not drop it."

"Ha-ha," I said. "You're funny, Mom."

"Did Cory win?" she asked.

I shook my head. "No. Laura. But Cory got a free ice-cream sundae."

"Lucky," Mom said.

The magic word.

"That reminds me," Mom said. "We need a birthday gift for Cory. His party is next Saturday. What do you think we should get him?"

I shrugged. "I don't know. He *thinks* he's getting a Wii from his parents. Maybe we could buy him a game."

"Well . . . you think about it," Mom said. She turned and headed downstairs.

I didn't think about it at all. I had homework to do and other things to think about.

Cory was a hard person to buy presents for. Because his parents always bought him everything he wanted. Lucky, right?

Later that night, it was time to change into my pajamas and go to sleep. I pulled pajamas from the dresser drawer. I guess I wasn't paying attention because I slammed the drawer on my hand.

"YEOOWWWWWW."

I shook my hand frantically. The pain just wouldn't quit!

Were my fingers broken? Did I crack my wrist?

"That stupid claw!" I cried out loud. "It has to go. I'm going to have bad luck until I get rid of it."

I grabbed the claw. I pulled it out from beneath the T-shirts.

Squeezing it in my fist, I held it in front of me and strode to the open bedroom window.

"Good-bye, claw," I muttered. "Good-bye and good riddance."

I raised it high. Pulled back my arm. And prepared to toss it out the window, toss it as far as I could.

But I stopped with my arm raised high.

I stopped, suddenly frozen like a statue. My mind was spinning.

I lowered my arm. My heart thudded. I took a deep breath.

I gazed at the black, feathery claw.

"Perfect," I murmured. "It's perfect. The perfect birthday gift for Cory."

I laughed. What a totally sweet idea.

"Here you go, Cory. I brought you a really nifty good-luck charm."

Ha-ha.

"Happy birthday, Lucky Duck."

I kissed the claw good-bye. Then I found a small box, tucked the claw inside, and wrapped a red ribbon around it.

22

On Saturday, Dad dropped me off at Cory's house for the birthday party. As I carried the claw to Cory's house, I felt a little bad. I knew it was a dirty trick to give him the bad-luck charm.

But Cory had all the good luck for too long. Why couldn't it be *my* turn for a while?

I knew that giving Cory a little bad luck was the only way I could win that Sports Camp scholarship. I gazed at the nicely wrapped package in my hand.

It's the Birthday Party of No Return for Cory, I thought.

This is where everything changes.

But I had a funny feeling in my stomach as I rang the doorbell. *I just hope Cory's bad luck isn't TOO bad,* I told myself.

Mrs. Duckworth opened the door. Cory looks a lot like his mom. The same blond hair and blue eyes. And she has the dimple on her chin, too.

"Hi, Lee." She stepped aside so I could walk in. "Everyone is downstairs. Just follow the noise."

Cory's basement is a giant playroom. That's where the family hangs out. They have a huge flat screen TV down there and shelves of books and board games and every toy Cory ever owned in his life. Tables and a bar with a real soda dispenser that has about six different kinds of soda pop. Lots of stereo equipment and a real karaoke machine.

I mean, it's everything you'd want all in one huge room.

And it was packed with kids now. I recognized just about every kid from school, and some cousins of Cory's I'd met before, and I saw a bunch of kids I didn't know.

"Hey, how's it going, Lee?" Cory greeted me. We bumped knuckles. He was wearing faded cargo jeans and a red and black T-shirt that said BIRTHDAY DUDE in big letters.

"Happy birthday," I said. I waved my present in front of him.

"Just add it to the pile," Cory said. He pointed to a card table stacked high with brightly wrapped presents.

I dropped my present on the pile. I had that funny feeling in my stomach again. *Stop thinking about it*, I scolded myself. *He deserves a little bad luck.*

I turned and gazed around the room. Kids were having a great time. Music thundered. I spotted Laura with some other girls, all carrying plates with pizza slices.

"My parents gave me a Wii," Cory said. "Check it out." He pointed to the big TV against the wall.

A bunch of kids were huddled around it. Gray Haddox was playing tennis. He was swinging the controller hard, killing each serve.

A tall blue and white iced birthday cake, loaded with candles, stood beside the food table. I walked over and grabbed a handful of tortilla chips.

"Awesome party," I told Cory, shouting over the music.

Some guys had found a soccer ball and were batting it back and forth across the room. A few girls had turned on the karaoke machine. But you couldn't hear them over the roaring music.

I hung out with some guys for a while, just goofing and talking about stuff. There was a huge bouquet of balloons floating near the stairway. Some guys thought it was funny to pop them and make kids scream.

Suddenly, the music stopped. Mrs. Duckworth strode across the room. "Time for Cory to open his presents," she announced.

She dragged a big trash can up to the table. "Put the wrapping paper in here," she told Cory. "Everyone gather around."

We all huddled in front of the gift table, dropping onto the couches, chairs, and the floor. A few kids kept playing Wii. The sounds of the game rang off the low ceiling.

With his mom watching from the side, Cory began opening presents. He wasn't careful with the wrapping paper or anything. He just ripped the packages open with both hands.

"Sweet! Sweet!" he kept exclaiming, holding up each present.

He got a lot of books and funny T-shirts and Wii games. Someone gave him a huge box of Starburst candy, his favorite.

He was about halfway through the presents when he picked mine up.

"Is this from you, Lee?" he asked.

I nodded. "Yeah."

I suddenly felt really nervous. My hands went cold and I could feel my neck muscles tighten.

I held my breath as Cory ripped away the red ribbon, then the wrapping paper. Then he jerked open the box.

He pulled out the vulture claw and lifted it high for everyone to see.

"Sweet!" he cried. "Check it out. A good-luck charm."

He turned to me with a smile on his face. "Thanks a lot, Lee," he said. "But I already have one of these."

23

"Huh?" I let out a loud gasp.

Cory set down the vulture claw. He reached under his BIRTHDAY DUDE T-shirt. And he pulled up a vulture claw he had around his neck.

"See?" he said. "Why do you think I've been even luckier than usual?" He waved the claw at me. "This thing really works."

He tucked his claw back under his shirt. Then he picked up my claw and tossed it back to me.

I was totally in shock. But somehow I caught it in both hands. I shoved it in my pocket.

Cory walked over to me. "You keep it, dude," he said. "You need good luck, too." He gave me a playful punch in the side. "But thanks anyway for such an awesome gift. You're a great friend."

Before I could say anything, he walked back

to the table and started to rip open more presents.

I'm a great friend?

What's up with this? This is supposed to be the Birthday Party of No Return for Cory.

But it turns out he has his own good-luck claw. And now I have my unlucky one back.

I had no choice. I had to take it back.

I couldn't concentrate on the rest of the gifts. My head was spinning. I could only think about the two claws.

Why was Cory's claw lucky and my claw unlucky? Was it really Arfy's fault? How could I make the claw lucky again?

Could I buy another one? I didn't have a clue about where this one came from.

I shut my eyes. I had to force myself to stop thinking about the claws. I wanted to enjoy the party.

I walked over to the Wii game. About ten or twelve kids were gathered in front of the big TV. They were still playing the tennis game.

I waited my turn. Then I took the controller.

"I hope this is easy," I said. "I haven't played this before."

I gripped the controller tightly. Stared at the screen. Readied myself . . .

The serve came at me. I swung hard.

I gasped as the controller slid from my hand and sailed toward the TV screen.

"Nooo!" I moaned over the crash. "Oh, no. Oh, no."

I raised my hands to the sides of my face. "It was an accident!" I cried. "An *accident*!"

24

The controller shot into the center of the TV screen. A deafening crash. The glass shattered into dozens of jagged cracks. Like a spiderweb over the screen. Then shards of glass dropped to the floor.

Kids cried out and jumped back. Everyone turned to stare at me.

"An accident!" I cried. "It . . . slipped!"

I didn't like their angry stares. They were upset they wouldn't get to play the Wii anymore. I'd ruined their fun.

I saw Mrs. Duckworth hurrying across the room. "What happened?" she cried. "What was that crash?"

I just wanted to shrink into the floor. I knew my face was burning red.

I backed away. I wanted to get as far away as I could.

I should have watched where I was going.

I felt a *bump* on my back. It startled me, and I stumbled backward.

"Oh, noooo," I moaned.

I backed into the food table. I felt it jolt. I turned in time to see the table tilt — and tumble onto its side.

Plates and bowls and platters and glasses slid to the floor. Pizza slices made a sick plop. Glasses shattered. Chips flew everywhere. Spilled soda formed a lake under the overturned table.

"No! No way! No way!" Mrs. Duckworth shouted.

I tried to step away from the mess. But my legs were acting crazy.

I slipped on a pizza slice. My hands flew up as I fell back —

— and landed on the birthday cake.

"Whoooaaa." A cry escaped my throat as I fell on top of the cake. Crashed to the floor. Sprawled on my back. Helpless with the gooey cake beneath me.

I rolled off the cake with a groan. Blue and white icing stuck to my shirt and the back of my pants.

I tried to wipe it off, but clumps of icing stuck to my hands. My face itched. I tried to scratch it and icing smeared my cheeks.

I glimpsed myself in the wall mirror. Blue and white icing covered my hair.

Everyone in the room was going nuts. Kids were shouting and shrieking and running around. Cory stood in the broken glass from the

TV screen, staring at the mess from the fallen food table. Staring. Just staring.

I tried to brush icing off my pants. I felt someone grab my shoulder. Hard.

I looked up to see Mrs. Duckworth. Her face was red. She had her jaw clenched. I swear I could see fire shooting from her eyes.

She squeezed my shoulder until I cried out. "Come with me, Lee," she said through gritted teeth.

Across the room, a girl slipped on the sticky spilled soda and fell onto a pile of pizza slices. Kids were still shouting and shaking their heads in disbelief.

Mrs. Duckworth led me up the basement stairs, away from the party. "Don't touch anything," she said. "I'm warning you — don't touch anything. I don't want icing all over my house."

"S-sorry," I stammered.

We reached the kitchen. She let go of my shoulder and turned to face me. She studied me from head to foot. "Are you okay, Lee? You're not hurt?"

"I — I'm okay, I guess," I murmured. I brushed a lump of icing off my cheek. But then I didn't know where to put it. So I wiped it on my jeans.

"I'm calling your parents," Mrs. Duckworth said. "To come pick you up."

"Okay," I said softly.

"You ruined Cory's party," she said, squinting hard at me. "You didn't do all that to be funny — did you?"

I swallowed. My throat was suddenly very dry. "Funny?" I squeaked. "No. I —"

"So it wasn't deliberate?" she asked.

I shook my head. "No way. It was an accident. Really."

"It was a *lot* of accidents," she said. She made a face. Like she had just bitten into a really sour lemon.

"I — I'm sorry," I stuttered.

"I mean, it's hard to destroy a TV, knock over a heavy food table, and sit on a birthday cake," she said. "Very hard to do all that."

I nodded. "Just bad luck," I muttered. I didn't know what else to say. Then I added, "I didn't sit on the cake. I fell on it."

She made a *hmpf* sound. Then she picked up a phone and called my house.

I sighed. How could she think I did all that on purpose?

Cory is my friend. I would never deliberately ruin his birthday party. Never.

My mom pulled up in the car five minutes later. She let out a cry when she saw me. I told her I was okay. I said I had an accident with the cake. I said I'd explain later.

Mom apologized at least twenty times to Mrs. Duckworth.

"It was quite *unusual*," Mrs. Duckworth said. She kept using the word *unusual*. Then she excused herself. "I have a lot of cleaning up to do."

Cory came upstairs to say good-bye. I told him I was sorry that I wrecked his party.

I pulled him into the front hall. "It's the claw," I said. I whispered so my mom wouldn't hear. She was still in the kitchen. She was on her phone, calling Dad.

Cory stared hard at me. "What about the claw?"

"Mine is different from yours," I said. "Something bad happened to it. Now it's *bad* luck all the time."

I sighed. "Everything that just happened downstairs? The mess I made? All because of the claw. It gives me bad luck instead of good."

Cory shook his head. "Lee — didn't you read the instructions?"

25

Instructions?

I had a sudden flash. I remembered opening the box the claw came in. And I pictured the small, square sheet of paper that fluttered out of the box.

Arfy grabbed it and ran away with it.

Were those the instructions?

"Come with me," Cory said. He started to grab my sleeve. But he pulled his hand away when he saw the sleeve was smeared with cake icing.

I followed him to his bedroom. He had rock posters all over his walls, from floor to ceiling. Some of them belonged to his parents and went all the way back to the 1970s. Very cool.

"I think I still have the instruction sheet that came with my claw," Cory said. He began pawing through a desk drawer.

"Yes. Here." He pulled out a square white sheet of paper and handed it to me. "You didn't read this?" he asked.

I shook my head. "No. My dog took it and ate it."

My eyes scanned the page of small type. There weren't many instructions. But I gasped when I found the one important rule:

"This rare vulture claw will bring you good luck forever," I read. *"But you must follow one rule. You must never KISS the claw. Kissing it is forbidden."*

"Oh, wow," I murmured. "Oh, wow."

I stared at those words. I read them again. My heart started to pound like crazy. I suddenly felt cold all over.

I kept reading:

"If you kiss the claw, your luck will turn bad. And you will have very bad dreams, and your whole life will turn into a nightmare."

The instruction sheet trembled in my hand. I shut my eyes. I pictured myself kissing the claw. Many times.

When I opened my eyes, Cory was staring hard at me. "You kissed your claw — didn't you?" he said.

I nodded. "A lot," I muttered.

"Bad luck," Cory said.

"Yeah. Bad luck," I said. "Bad luck all the time." I sighed again. "Where did you get your claw?"

He shrugged. "Beats me. It just came in the mail."

"Me, too," I said. "Wish I'd read the instructions."

"Lee? Where are you?" Mom called from the kitchen. "We have to go!"

"Coming!" I shouted. I started toward the bedroom door. But Cory grabbed my arm.

"I just want to ask you one more question," he said.

I turned and waited for him to ask it.

"Why did you give your claw to me as a birthday present?" he asked. "To give me bad luck?"

My mouth dropped open. I could feel my face grow hot, and I knew I was blushing.

"Sorry," I said. "It was a stupid idea. I . . . I didn't want you to have *real* bad luck." I shook my head. "Really. I'm sorry."

His eyes went cold. He blew out a long whoosh of air. "Kind of a dirty trick," he said. "You're supposed to be my friend."

I opened my mouth to answer. But my eyes went to the open window.

The sky darkened suddenly. I saw an ugly creature soar toward the window. It filled the window. Huge. Let out a raw bleating sound.

An enormous gray and black vulture.

It stepped onto the window ledge, cawing loudly. It raised one leg. *The leg had no claw at the end!*

Just a black stump. A ragged, ugly bump.

I uttered a cry as the huge bird lowered its head — and bolted into the room.

"Look out!" I screamed.

No time to duck. Or run.

It raised its wings high. Lowered its massive beak — and dove at me.

26

I screamed and covered my head.

Cory laughed. "I'm not going to hit you," he said. "You don't have to duck."

I blinked. I lowered my arms. I gazed at Cory. He stood staring at me, a puzzled expression on his face.

"Lee — what was *that* about?"

"Well . . . I . . ."

No ugly bleating vulture in the room.

I was seeing things again. Another hallucination. I should have known.

"Are you okay?" Cory asked.

My whole body was trembling. "Not really," I said. "This claw is messing up my brain." I reached into my pocket and felt the claw. "I have to get rid of it."

He nodded. "Yeah. As fast as you can."

I apologized again for wrecking his birthday party. And for trying to pass off the bad-luck claw to him. Then I hurried to the kitchen to find Mom.

"So what happened, Lee?" Mom asked as we drove home. "What went wrong at the party?"

"Everything," I replied. How could I explain?

Both hands on the steering wheel, Mom turned to stare at me. "Maybe you could describe it a little better than that?"

"I really can't," I said. "I — I smashed his TV. Then I fell. And I knocked the food over. And then I fell again — on the cake. It was all a horrible accident."

"Were you dizzy?" Mom asked. "Should we take you to Dr. Markoff?"

"No. I told you — it was an accident," I said.

Mom nodded. She gazed out the windshield and bit her bottom lip. She only bites her lip like that when she's worried.

I stared out the car window. We passed a group of kids on bikes. They grinned at me and raised their arms. They all had claws instead of hands.

"Oh, noooo," I muttered.

A scrawny gray and black vulture landed on the hood of the car. It stared at me through the windshield. Then it raised an ugly, clawless stump at me.

I'm living a nightmare! I thought. *I can't tell what's real and what isn't real.*

My life would never return to normal until I got rid of that horrible claw.

Mom pulled the car up our driveway. I pushed open my door and bolted out, eager to get going.

"There's something I have to do," I said.

"Yes, there is," Mom replied. "You have to walk Arfy."

"Huh?" I started to protest. But Mom pushed me toward the house.

"Give Arfy a good long walk," she said. "He's been lying around the house all day. He needs some exercise."

"But, Mom —"

"No arguing," she said. "Some fresh air will do you good, too."

No, it won't, I told myself. *Fresh air won't change my luck. Fresh air won't stop these frightening hallucinations.*

I stepped into the house first. Arfy was waiting. The big sheepdog leaped onto me and tackled me to the floor. Then he wrapped me in a headlock and planted wet tongue kisses all over my face.

I screamed. He had a vulture head. He was licking me . . . licking me with a disgusting, scratchy vulture tongue!

"Noooo!" I rolled out from under him and jumped to my feet. His head was back to normal now. I grabbed his leash off the hook by the back door. I hooked Arfy up, and we headed out the door.

The late afternoon sun was dipping behind the trees. Long shadows stretched across the front yards. Trees shimmered with their fresh leaves.

"Whoa!" I let out a cry as Arfy started to run. "Slow down! Hey — take it slower!"

The big guy had been cooped up all day. I could see he wanted to stretch his legs. He wanted to *run*.

But I wanted to take it slow. I needed to be careful, to watch out for more hallucinations.

"Arfy — stop!" I shouted. "Arfy — stay! Stay, boy!"

He gave the leash a hard tug and bounded into the middle of the street. I tried to pull him back onto the sidewalk. But he was a lot stronger than me.

"Arfy — stop! Stop!"

He lowered his furry head and plowed on, picking up speed. Running down the middle of the street.

"Arfy — no!"

I heard a *snap*. The leash flew back and hit me in the chest. Arfy kept running.

Running *free*!

The leash had snapped off, and Arfy was on the loose.

"Stop! STOP!" I screamed.

This was not a hallucination. This was *real*. The dog kept running full speed, his four legs pounding the street pavement.

I chased after him, running as fast as I could. But the big dog was galloping now. My legs ached. My heart throbbed. I couldn't catch up.

"Arfy — please!" I wailed breathlessly. "Please stop!" I was in a total panic now.

I didn't see the black car. I only heard the squeal of tires.

A horn blared right behind me. So close and so loud that I screamed.

The tires squealed.

WHUMMMP.

The car hit me from behind.

I felt the bump at the bottom of my back. It didn't feel very strong.

But it sent me flying.

I didn't really have time to know what was happening.

I landed hard on my back a few feet away.

I died instantly.

27

No. I was alive. I didn't die.

I didn't even come close to dying. It was hard to believe but I actually wasn't hurt at all. Not a scrape.

I opened my eyes. I was sprawled flat on the pavement. Arfy stood over me. He lowered his head and began licking my face.

A small, dark-haired woman in a short black jacket and black skirt stood staring down at me. She had her hands balled into tense fists. Her whole body was trembling.

"You — you're okay?" Her voice came out in a whisper. "Should I call for an ambulance?"

I moved my arms and legs. I sat up. "I'm okay," I said. "I feel fine."

She let out a long whoosh of air. "I'm so glad," she said. "I couldn't stop in time. You ran right out in front of me."

"I was chasing after my dog," I said. I held on to Arfy's leather collar.

"Can you stand?" The woman reached to help me up. "Does anything hurt? Want me to drive you home?"

Her hands on my shoulders were ice-cold. Her whole body still shook.

I let her pull me to my feet. I stretched, testing my arms and legs. I rolled my head around, testing my neck.

"I'm fine. It wasn't a hard bump," I told her. "No problem. Really."

She led me to her car. She insisted she had to drive me home.

I stuffed Arfy into the backseat. All the way home, I swore to her I felt fine. She pulled up the driveway and watched me lead Arfy into the house. She didn't leave till I closed the door.

Mom was waiting in the kitchen for me. "Lee, you got a phone message. From Coach Taylor. He said the tag football game is first thing tomorrow morning."

"Tomorrow?"

She nodded. "Is this the final competition for the scholarship?"

"Yes," I said. "It's my last chance."

"Do or die," Mom said.

I wished she hadn't put it that way.

"I know you'll be a star," she added. She patted my shoulder. Then she made a face. "Ooh. What's that smell?"

I checked the bottom of my sneakers. "Oh,

noooo." I'd stepped in dog poop. Both sneakers were totally smeared with it.

No way I can be a star tomorrow, I thought. *No way I can escape this bad luck. My life is getting more and more dangerous. I was hit by a car because of the claw.*

What will happen next?

I knew I couldn't keep the claw another minute. I grabbed it and swung it around by the rope. Then I ran to the backyard.

Dad keeps our three trash cans behind the garage. I opened the first metal can and stuffed the claw inside it. Then I slammed the lid shut.

My heart was pounding. Sweat poured down my face. But I felt better already.

The claw was history. Time for my luck to change . . .

28

At dinner that night, I felt tense. I waited for something bad to happen.

Would I scald my mouth on the soup? Knock my spaghetti on the floor? Fall off my chair and break my neck?

When that didn't happen, it made me even more nervous.

I kept picturing the claw in the trash can behind the garage. Was it still too nearby? Could it still cause me all kinds of danger?

Dad wiped the spaghetti sauce off his chin and turned to me with a solemn expression. "I've got bad news, Lee," he said softly.

I gasped. "Wh-what?" I stammered.

A smile slowly crossed his face. "I could only get tickets in the second row for the Stampede game next Saturday night," he said.

Of course, he was making a joke.

"That's awesome!" I cried. "Second row. Wow!"

He nodded. "We'll have fun."

"Dad, what day do they pick up the trash?" I asked.

He squinted at me. "The trash? It's out back? Why?"

I shrugged. "Just wondering."

"Tomorrow, I think," Mom said. "Why on earth do you care about the trash, Lee?"

I had to think fast. "Uh . . . we're studying trash in school," I said.

Pretty good answer — right?

We had chocolate chip cookies for dessert. Just as we were finishing, the doorbell rang.

I shut my eyes. The sound sent a shiver down my back.

Was someone bringing bad news? Was my bad luck starting up again?

I hurried to the front door. Pulled it open — and let out a cry.

"Laura!" I exclaimed. "What are you doing here?"

She made a face at me. "Oh. Nice welcome. Thanks. Great to see you, too."

I could feel myself blushing. "But — But —" I sputtered. "I didn't expect —"

She rolled her eyes. "I texted you twice this afternoon. Don't you read your texts? I said I was coming over to fill out the science work sheets with you."

"Uh . . . *really*?"

I couldn't believe it. Laura came over to do homework with me. That was definitely good news.

Maybe . . . just maybe . . . the evil spell of the claw had ended.

She was wearing a yellow sweater over a blue T-shirt and dark jeans with silver studs around the pockets.

She pushed past me into the house, bumping me with her backpack. Mom and Dad greeted her from the dining room. She followed me in. Mom offered her some cookies.

I picked up a cookie, bit off a big chunk of it — and it went down the wrong pipe. I started to choke.

I made a horrible wheezing sound. I couldn't breathe in or out.

Dad slapped me hard on the back. A wet glob of cookie came flying out of my mouth and splatted the front of Laura's sweater.

She lifted it off with two fingers and set it down on a plate. "You're gross," she said.

"I think Arfy taught him how to eat," Dad said.

It was a joke. A really lame joke. But Laura laughed like it was a riot.

Did the claw make me choke? I asked myself. I pictured it in the trash can out back. *Was it still too nearby?*

Laura and I went into the den to fill out the science sheets. We sat down beside each other on the green leather couch and rested the papers on the coffee table in front of us.

I couldn't relax. I couldn't concentrate.

I was so totally ready for disaster.

Laura had to do most of the work.

The vulture claw was just too close to forget about.

"Hey, I was hit by a car this afternoon," I blurted out.

Laura gazed hard at me. "Ha!" she said. "I don't get it."

"It's not a joke," I said. "I was hit by a car. Really."

"And you got up and walked away?" she said. "Who are you supposed to be? Superman?"

"Never mind," I muttered. I could see she was not going to believe me.

Laura tapped her pencil on the coffee table. "You know, I'm playing in the football game tomorrow morning, too," she said.

"Yeah, I know," I replied. "So?"

"So you and Cory don't think that I have a chance — do you?"

"Of course you have a chance," I said. I groaned. "You're way ahead of me."

"You and Cory are both total weirdos," she said. She poked me in the stomach with the eraser end of her pencil.

"We are not!" I said. "Why are we weirdos?"

"Walking around wearing those ugly claw things?" she said, shaking her head. "I couldn't believe when you tried to give him one, and he already had one."

"Yeah. That was a *little* weird," I admitted. Then I added: "But I got rid of mine."

Laura's mouth dropped open. "Excuse me?"

"I dumped mine in the trash out back," I said. "It was bad news. I don't believe in good-luck charms."

She laughed. "You're going to *need* a good-luck charm at the game tomorrow. I'm going to *trash* both you guys."

We filled out the work sheets. I don't think glaciers are very interesting. But Miss Harrison must like them a lot. She keeps giving us assignment after assignment about the glaciers.

Laura and I had a few more cookies. In fact, we finished the plate. Then she went home. "Good luck tomorrow," she said as she stepped out the door.

I'll need it, I thought.

My last chance.

Later, I changed into my pajamas and got ready for bed. I felt restless. My stomach kept growling and groaning.

I knew I couldn't relax until the trash was picked up and the claw was carried away.

A soft breeze blew my curtains. I stepped up

to my window and gazed outside. My window faces the backyard. I could see Dad's vegetable garden.

The tomato plants tilted on their poles. A branch had fallen off the maple tree next to the garage. It lay in the grass, raised at one end like a fat snake.

Moonlight made the grass shimmer like silver. And . . . and . . .

What was that dark object slithering through the silver grass?

Like a dark glove scrabbling toward the house.

I stared down at it, frozen in terror. I watched it slide and crawl through the bright moonlight.

The claw. The claw . . . *crawling back*.

"Nooooooo." I sent a horrified howl out the window. "Nooooooo."

29

I spun away from the window and took a deep breath. I could feel the blood pulsing at my temples.

This can't be happening.

This is impossible.

The claw was crawling to the house, bringing its bad luck back to me.

Returning so that it could ruin my chances tomorrow morning.

No. No way!

Before I realized what I was doing, I was running barefoot down the stairs. The house was dark. Mom and Dad must have been sound asleep.

I was in my pajamas, but I didn't care. I burst out the kitchen door and ran into the backyard. My bare feet slipped and slid on the wet, dewy grass.

A cool breeze blew against my hot face. My pajama shirt fluttered like a kite in the wind.

White moonlight poured over the lawn. The backyard gleamed, almost as bright as day.

Where is it? Where?

My eyes scanned the lawn as I ran. I had to find it.

What would I do with it when I did? Heave it as far as I could?

I jumped over the fallen tree limb. The old maple tree creaked and groaned in the strong breeze.

In the bright moonlight, I could see every weed, every blade of grass.

And there it was! The dark claw! Scrabbling slowly . . . so slowly . . . through the wet grass.

I stopped, my heart pounding so hard that my chest ached. My knees nearly folded. I took another deep breath, trying to steady myself.

Then I lowered myself to take a closer look at the crawling claw.

"Oh, wow," I murmured out loud. "Oh, wow."

Not the claw.

It wasn't the claw. It was a small box turtle. Its square shell dark against the shimmering grass.

A box turtle. Crawling slowly over the backyard.

A laugh escaped my throat. I wanted to cheer. But that might wake up my parents.

A light was on in the kitchen window next door. Did the neighbors see me out here in my pajamas?

Would they think it was weird that I ran out late at night to stare at a box turtle?

Well, yes, it was weird. But my life had been weird lately.

No more. No more weirdness, I told myself.

I turned to the trash cans behind the garage. The lids were all tightly clamped shut. The claw was safe inside its can.

As I stared, the metal cans made a rattling sound.

I started to panic. But I caught myself. And laughed again.

They were rattling because of the wind.

It had to be the wind. Right?

30

Early the next morning, I dropped my backpack in my gym locker and started to get dressed for the football competition.

It was only tag football. But Coach Taylor made everyone wear full equipment — knee pads, shoulder pads, and a helmet.

I tried on three helmets, and they were all too big for me. I never knew I had such a tiny head! Finally, I just took one of the big ones. I figured it was no big deal if it slipped around a little.

Some of the guys were goofing on one another, making jokes and bumping one another into the lockers. But I stayed quiet in my corner of the locker room. I wanted to concentrate.

This was the most important game of my life.

Cory came in when I was almost in my uniform. He tossed his backpack against the wall and set his helmet down on the bench. He started to unlock his locker.

"How's it going, Lee?" he asked.

"Not bad," I said. "Actually, I feel good. I feel good about this game."

"Me, too," he said.

He pulled off his T-shirt and stuffed it in the locker. Then he lifted the good-luck claw off his neck. He set it down on the bench beside the helmet.

"I'm going to the Stampede game at the arena Saturday," Cory said. He struggled with the shoulder pads. Realized he had them on backward. Took them off and started again.

"I get to sit on the bench and hang out with the players," he said.

"I'm going to the game, too," I told him. "My dad got tickets in the second row."

"Awesome," Cory said. He tightened the shoulder-pad straps. "Maybe I could get a ride with you, Lee. My parents are going somewhere Saturday night, and they didn't want to drive me."

"Sure," I said. "I'll tell my dad to stop at your house."

Yes, we were in a competition to the death. But Cory and I were still friends. It was a *friendly* competition.

Except . . . staring at his vulture claw on the bench, I suddenly didn't feel so friendly.

I mean, it wasn't fair. Really.

I mean, I was happy I got rid of my bad luck. But Cory still had his *good*-luck charm. Cory still had all the good luck.

That meant I was going to lose today. Lose the game and lose my last chance for the scholarship.

"Anything wrong?" Cory's question broke into my thoughts.

"No. No problem," I said. I grabbed the big helmet and started to pull it over my hair. "This thing weighs a ton."

Cory started to answer. But Coach Taylor stepped up to his locker. "Cory, would you do me a favor? I left my playbook in my office on the second floor. Would you run up and get it for me?"

"Sure," Cory said. He pulled a jersey down over the shoulder pads. Then he took off toward the locker-room door.

I set my helmet back on the bench. I saw that I hadn't tightened the laces on my football cleats. I sat down and started to work on them.

My eyes stopped on the object on the floor. A claw. Cory's claw. He didn't put it back. It must have fallen off the bench.

My brain started to whir. Thoughts flashed through my mind like comets. All kinds of thoughts. Including *evil* thoughts.

The claw sat inches away from me. I gazed around. No one was looking. Most of the other guys had already run out to the football field.

I picked up Cory's claw. I rubbed my fingers over it.

Should I do it? Should I?

I couldn't resist.

Cory was my friend. But I really needed to outplay him today.

I raised the claw to my mouth and kissed it.

Then I turned it over and kissed the back.

Then I kissed both sides again. Then I planted kisses all over it.

All those kisses got it a little wet. I dried it off on the front of my football jersey. Then I placed it back on the floor exactly where it had fallen.

Did I feel bad about what I just did?

Not really. If the claw brought Cory a little bad luck this afternoon, it would just even things up. You know. Make it more fair.

I pulled the helmet over my head and started to the door. Cory burst in, and we almost collided.

"Good game," he said.

"You, too," I said.

We bumped knuckles. And I trotted out to the field.

31

Coach Taylor divided us up into Team Offense and Team Defense. After ten or fifteen minutes, we switched teams.

Cory and Laura played on Team Offense at first. I was on Team Defense.

I readied myself. Clenched my jaw. Tightened every muscle. I was totally psyched.

I leaned into position and stretched my arms out at my sides. No one was going to get past me. No one.

Cory started as quarterback for Team Offense. On the first play, he handed the ball to Gray Haddox. Gray burst through the line for a few yards. Then he was swarmed on and tagged by three or four players on my team.

On the next play, Cory dropped back to pass. I shot through the line, waving my hands above my head. I grabbed him around the waist. "You're tagged."

Coach Taylor blew his whistle. He pointed at me. "No tackling!"

I shrugged my shoulder pads. "That was a tag," I said.

I felt good. Taylor saw how enthusiastic I was. And he saw me make a really good play on Cory.

One point for Lee Hargrove.

The coach whistled for us to start play again.

This time, Cory kept the ball and ran to the other side, away from me. I rocketed across the field. Reached out for him . . . reached . . .

. . . And just missed him.

He ran for a touchdown.

Score one for Lucky Duckworth.

Cory's team took the ball on offense again. Some kids had gathered on the sidelines to watch the contest.

I leaned into my defensive stance. I readied myself. *Focus*, I told myself. *Stay alert. Focus. You can do this. You can win this.*

Cory tossed the ball to Laura. She tore through the line, zigzagged like crazy, and ran for about twenty yards.

Not bad. Especially for a girl.

There were four girls in the game. Four girls trying for the scholarship. All of them had done pretty well in bowling and tennis. But Laura was the best of the four.

Did she have a chance to win and go to Sports Camp?

Well, yes. She had a chance. Of course, she had a small chance.

Did I still have a chance? If I made a few more really awesome plays, the answer would be yes.

I'd score some points with Coach Taylor for playing well. And if I could score enough sportsmanship points and Most Improved points, I could definitely win the prize.

I tensed myself. Forced myself to breathe slowly, steadily. Kept my eyes moving.

Superstar time. All-pro time. KILLER time.

On the next play, Cory kept the ball. He cut left, then cut right. He had the ball tucked tightly under his arm and his helmet lowered. And he was thundering in a straight line — right at me!

I stuck out my arms. Lowered my helmet. Tightened my stance.

Ready to tag him. Ready for him as he ran toward me. Ready.

"OWWWWWWWWOOOOOO."

Was that *me* shrieking like that? Did I hear *him* shrieking, too?

The pain rocketed from my head down my body. A tidal wave of throbbing, hammering pain.

Everything went black even before I hit the ground.

32

"What happened?"

My voice came out in a hoarse whisper. I struggled to see but everything was a blur. It hurt to raise my head. I lowered it to the grass.

Someone had removed my helmet. It lay a few feet away from me.

"Am I alive?" I croaked.

Coach Taylor appeared above me. "I think you're okay. Let's try to sit you up."

He pushed me from behind. I groaned. But the pain was starting to fade.

The ground tilted down. The trees beyond the playground wouldn't come into focus.

I saw Cory sitting across from me, his legs spread. His helmet was off, and he kept shaking his head.

"Whoa," he murmured. "Whoa."

"What happened?" I asked Coach Taylor. "Was it an earthquake or something?"

"You two butted heads," Taylor said. "You went down and Laura picked up the ball and scored a touchdown."

I squinted past him. Laura stood in a line with the other players. She still had the football in her hands. Everyone looked really frightened. No one made a sound.

"We have to check you two out for concussions," Taylor said. "Do you think you can walk back into the school?"

It took a while to stand up. My head throbbed. I was totally dizzy.

Cory took a few staggering steps. I could see he was dizzy, too.

Coach Taylor helped us both into the locker room. "Get changed," he said. "I'm taking you to a doctor to get you checked out."

Cory and I grunted replies.

"Sorry, guys," Taylor said. "That collision was really bad luck." He turned and headed back outside.

Bad luck.

The words rang in my spinning, pulsing head. *Bad luck.*

Well, I knew why Cory had bad luck. I gave it to him by kissing his vulture claw. I turned his claw into a bad-luck charm.

But . . . why did I have such bad luck? I had thrown the claw in the trash.

"Do you have your phone?" Cory asked. He rubbed his eyes. "I want to call my mom and tell her we're going to see the doctor."

"Sure," I said. I pulled my backpack out of the locker. I unzipped it and reached inside.

I knew my cell phone was somewhere near the bottom.

I fumbled around, pushing stuff out of the way.

My hand wrapped around something tucked between two textbooks.

I pulled it out — and stared in shock at my vulture claw.

33

The doctor checked out Cory and me and said we were okay. No concussions. He said we might have headaches for a while.

My headache got worse. I couldn't stop thinking about the claw. Of course, one question kept repeating in my mind: *How did it get from the trash can to the bottom of my backpack?*

It was all I could think about. And I couldn't come up with an answer.

I was still thinking about it on the morning of the Awards Assembly at school.

Our school has the Awards Assembly in the auditorium every spring near the end of the school year. All kinds of awards are given out. Sports awards, academic awards, public service awards. There is even an award for the Best Smile.

It was a tense morning for me. Because the winner of the Sports Camp scholarship was also being announced.

Cory and I sat together near the back of the auditorium. We were both too tense to talk.

I knew I hadn't played well enough to win. But maybe I stood a chance. Maybe I scored points for Desire, and Enthusiasm, and Sportsmanship, and Improvement.

Those could put me over the top.

Cory and I kept glancing at each other as the awards were handed out and kids came to the stage to accept them. I could see that he was just as stressed as I was.

We sat twitching and squirming through the Mayor's Trophy for Most Litter Picked Up on the Playground. And the award for Loudest Singer in Music Class.

I couldn't sit still. My hands were sweaty and cold. My stomach kept growling and doing flip-flops.

I nearly jumped when Ms. Lincoln, our principal, announced it was time to reveal the Sports Camp scholarship winner.

I held my breath. I glanced at Cory. He had gone pale.

"We have three finalists," Ms. Lincoln said. "I'd like to call all three to the stage now."

I still hadn't taken a breath. I was too tense to breathe!

The principal read the list of names into the microphone: "Cory Duckworth . . . Laura Grodin . . . and . . ."

And?

". . . Lee Hargrove."

Yes!

I let my breath out in a long whoosh. My legs trembled as I climbed up from my seat and started down the long aisle to the stage.

Cory stopped me in the wings. "Here. Take this," he said. "For luck."

He pulled his vulture claw off and draped it around my neck.

"No. Please —" I gasped. I tried to shove it back to him.

"You need it more than I do," Cory said. "You're my best friend. I know how much you want this. Maybe it'll bring you luck."

I frantically tried to hand the claw back to him. He didn't know that I had kissed it. He was trying to do a nice thing. He didn't know it was *bad* luck now.

"Cory — take it back!" I cried. "Please —"

I glanced up at the stage. Ms. Lincoln was staring down at us. She didn't look happy.

"Cory? Lee? What's your problem?" she demanded. "You both have stage fright?"

The whole auditorium burst into laughter.

I had no choice. I followed Cory onto the stage. The bad-luck claw hung heavy on my neck. No way to give it back to him.

So there we were. Cory, Laura, and I standing in a line onstage in front of the whole school.

Talk about *awkward*. I couldn't decide where to put my hands. Finally, I jammed them into my jeans pockets.

The vulture claw dangled over my chest. I wanted to rip it off and toss it away.

But how could I? Cory wouldn't understand. He would never forgive me.

The principal was saying something about how sorry she was she had only one scholarship to hand out. I couldn't really hear her. I couldn't hear anything over the beating of my heart.

Just tell us who won! I thought. *Don't make a speech.*

Please tell us the winner!

Was Cory as nervous as me? I turned to him — and gasped.

I took a staggering step back.

As I stared in horror, Cory's face . . . his whole body started to change.

Black feathers poked out of his arms. Feathers uncurled all over his skin.

His body shifted and grew taller. His neck stretched as his head appeared to tighten . . . tighten like a fist.

His blue eyes disappeared into his face. His mouth vanished, too. Vanished under black feathers. And a long, curved beak poked out of his head.

His jeans dropped away. I could see his feathery legs. Thick gray and black feathers covered his whole body. His arms folded up. Folded into wide, flapping wings.

Cory opened his beak in a long, hoarse honk.

His body grew until he loomed over me. I stood frozen in his shadow. The shadow of a gigantic vulture.

He squawked again. The sound sent chills to the back of my neck.

Then Cory lowered his vulture head. Two tiny black eyes glared at me from over the long, curved beak. The beak opened and snapped at my face.

Snapped. Snapped again. Ripped at my cheeks. He raised his huge wings and dove for my throat.

I raised both arms to shield myself. Did he plan to tear me apart?

I staggered back. I opened my beak and let out a shrill squawk of rage. I raised my wings and —

Huh?

I lowered my gaze. I shrieked my surprise. I was a vulture, too. I had changed without even realizing it. Without even *feeling* it!

I narrowed my eyes at the Cory vulture. My feathers stood on end. I stretched my wings back and lowered my head. Ready to attack.

He dove at me. But I dodged to the side. I drove my sharp beak deep into his throat.

He raised his head in a hoarse cry of pain. Then he leaped high and shot his talons into my feathered chest.

It knocked me off-balance. I toppled onto my side, and he dove on top of me.

We wrestled on the stage floor, squawking and tearing at each other.

I could hear the horrified screams and cries of the kids in the auditorium.

This is going to be an assembly they'll never forget! I thought.

Cory ripped at my chest feathers with his sharp talons. I gave a hard twist — and shoved him off me.

Then I opened my beak and aimed for his throat.

Got to kill him! I told myself. *Only way to win this fight. Kill! KILL!*

34

A week later, Cory and I were walking down my street. School was over, and we were still getting used to having the whole day free.

It was a warm day. The air smelled like fresh-cut grass. Bright green leaves were starting to open on the trees.

Cory laughed and shook his head. "I can't believe you and I had a wrestling match on the auditorium stage."

"In front of the whole school," I added. "Did you see the look on Ms. Lincoln's face? She was so shocked, she froze. She couldn't move!"

"I didn't see her," Cory said. "I was too busy trying to fight you off."

We both laughed. We had to laugh about it. Otherwise, it would be too embarrassing.

"We actually tried to kill each other," I said. "I totally thought you had turned into a giant vulture."

"How weird is that?" Cory said. "I didn't know why you were fighting me. I just thought you freaked out."

"We were lucky it was the last week of school," I said. "Otherwise, we would have been sent home. Suspended."

We walked another block in silence. Some kids were tossing a red Frisbee in front of a house on the corner. Two dogs stood in the driveway barking at each toss.

"How did you get rid of that claw?" Cory asked.

"Rode my bike to the other side of town and dropped them both in a sewer," I said.

"Huh? I gave you my claw. You tossed it away?" Cory said.

"Your claw was bad luck, too," I told him. "Didn't you figure that out? They were both bad luck."

"Hey — there's Laura," he said, pointing.

She stood at the bottom of her driveway. Next to her, I saw two suitcases, a rolled-up sleeping bag, and some other junk.

She waved as Cory and I walked closer. "How's it going?" she called.

We stopped at the edge of her driveway. I glanced down the street. "You waiting for the Sports Camp bus?"

She nodded. "I'm so excited."

"Yeah. You're going to have fun," I said.

I tried to sound cheerful. I didn't want her to think I was bitter about the whole thing.

But Laura only won the scholarship because Cory and I fought onstage and were disqualified.

The yellow camp bus rumbled up to us and stopped. A driver in a gray uniform climbed down and started to load Laura's stuff into the luggage compartment.

"Well, bye," she said. She started to the bus. "See you in the fall."

She started to climb on, then stopped. She turned to us with a grin. "By the way, how did those claws work out for you?"

"Huh?" I stared at her.

"You never figured out that I was the one who sent them to you guys?" Laura asked, still grinning.

"No way!" Cory and I cried together.

She laughed. "Before I sent them to you, I kissed them both. I kissed them all over. I knew you'd wear them. And I knew *I'd* have all the good luck."

Cory blinked. "You kissed them first? Then how come Lee and I had *good* luck for a while?"

Laura shrugged. "Beats me. I guess the kisses just take a while to kick in."

She turned to me. "And I'll bet you never guessed that I pulled the claw from your trash can that night. And I stuck it in your backpack before the football game the next morning."

I sighed. "No. I never guessed."

"Well, I really wanted to win," Laura said. "Sometimes you have to make your OWN luck — right?"

She climbed onto the camp bus. "Bye, guys!" she called. "Have an *awesome* summer!"

WELCOME BACK TO
THE HALL OF HORRORS

Well, Lee, that was a strange story with an unhappy ending — for *you*.

Actually, I think you were lucky. Lucky that you and Cory didn't rip each other to shreds with your beaks and claws.

Oh. But that was just a hallucination — right?

Good-luck charms can be very powerful. That's why I wear this black widow spider around my neck. So far, it has only bitten me *twice*.

That's lucky, right?

Thank you for bringing your story to me. I am the Story-Keeper. And I will keep your story here where it belongs. You know, here in the Hall of Horrors, There's Always Room for One More Scream.

You're going to <u>want</u> to see this!

Are you ready to *face* a brand-new nightmare?

1

"I don't want to go to Polly Martin's Halloween party," I said. "I'm twelve years old, and I think I should be allowed to decide what parties I want to go to."

I punched the couch cushion. "Polly gives the lamest parties on Earth. No. In the universe. Her parties are so lame, they give the word *lame* a bad name."

My friend Devin O'Bannon laughed. "You're funny, Lu-Ann."

"I'm not being funny!" I screamed. "I'm serious. Why should Halloween be ruined because —"

"You've been friends with Polly since kindergarten," Devin said. He jammed a handful of popcorn into his mouth.

"You sound like my mom," I grumbled. "Just because we've known each other forever doesn't mean we're friends."

Devin said something, but his mouth was so loaded with popcorn, I couldn't understand a word he said. What a slob. But that's okay. I mean, all my friends are jokers and weirdos.

Devin and I were sitting on opposite ends of the couch in my den. We both had our feet up on the coffee table. Devin kept scooping up handfuls of popcorn from the big bowl my mom made. Half of them went into his mouth, the other half on the couch and floor.

My side of the couch was clean. I don't like popcorn. I only like sweets. I knew there was a carton of rocky road ice cream in the freezer. But I was feeling too lazy to get up and get it. Too lazy and too upset.

"You know the other thing I hate about Polly's parties?" I said.

He grinned. "Besides *everything*?"

"She makes you pay," I said. "Five dollars a person. Why do we have to pay money to be bored? I can be bored just sitting here with you."

"Thanks, Lu-Ann. You're a pal."

You can tell by the way I tease Devin that I like him a lot.

"Five dollars," I muttered.

"Well, you know Polly. She's never seen a dollar bill she didn't like."

"Guess Polly's idea of a great party game," I said with a moan.

"Spin the Bottle?"

"No. Shut up. That's too exciting. Her idea of a good game is rubbing a balloon on your forehead until the static electricity makes it stick. Then seeing who can keep the balloon on his face the longest."

Devin laughed again. "Got any balloons? We could practice."

I gave him a hard shove. "Why do you keep laughing? It isn't funny."

He spit out an unpopped kernel. Then he stuck it on my nose.

I slapped his hand away. "You are so immature."

"I learned it from you."

"Could you be any less funny?"

"I could try."

I grabbed a handful of popcorn from the bowl and dropped it in his red, curly hair. He shook his head hard, sending popcorn flying all over the den.

As I said, I like Devin a lot. He's fun. Not like Polly Martin.

Polly is sweet and nice. Really. She's very smart and a total knockout with her big green eyes and dazzling smile. Like a toothpaste model or something.

Her problem is that she's soooo serious. All the time. I mean, she smiles sometimes, but I've never seen her laugh. She doesn't get jokes. She never knows when you're teasing her. She's into Green Power and saving the bald eagles and she's a vegetarian. You get the picture.

Not that there's anything wrong with all that. But I told you, my friends are all jokers and clowns and goof-offs. So it's hard to stay close friends with her.

"Why do you think being forced to go to Polly's Halloween party is so funny?" I asked Devin. "You have to go, too."

"No, I don't."

"Excuse me? Why don't you?"

His grin faded. He raised his eyes to the TV on the wall. We had it on with the sound off. The TV is always on in my house. Don't ask me why. There was some cooking contest on the screen, with teams of people scrambling to make cupcakes as fast as they could.

"Lu-Ann, you might think you're the unluckiest person in the universe," Devin said. "But I am. I would *kill* to go to Polly's Halloween party."

"You're joking, right?"

"I wish." He let out a sad sigh. "My Halloween is going to be a *lot* lamer than yours."

I stared at him, waiting for him to continue.

He brushed more popcorn from his hair. "Do you know how to spell *tragic*?"

"Of course I do. I didn't have to take first grade three times like you."

"I only took it twice," he said. "My life is tragic, Lu-Ann. My Halloween will be tragic. It's the perfect word."

Devin and I talk about perfect words some-times. He knows I want to be a writer when I'm older. I'm really good at thinking up stories. Everyone says I have an awesome imagination.

My mom says my imagination is *too* awe-some. She doesn't mean that in a nice way. She wishes I was more serious, like my little brother, Mitch.

"Don't keep me in suspense, creep," I said. "Just tell me what's so tragic."

"My dad bought a pumpkin farm," he said.

"Your dad isn't a farmer. He works at an insur-ance company. Oh. Sorry. I mean, he *worked* at an insurance company. I know he's been looking for work. But . . . pumpkins?"

Devin rolled his brown eyes. "Tell me about it. Actually, he just leased it. It's one of those Pick-Your-Own-Pumpkin places. You know. You walk in the field and pull your own pumpkins off the vine. Big thrill, right?"

"We did that when I was five," I said. "I thought those long, twisty vines were creepy. Mitch was two and he started to cry. So we had to leave."

"I'm going to cry, too," Devin said. "But Dad thinks he's going to make a fortune selling pump-kins. It's only one week till Halloween. How many pumpkins can he sell?"

I shook my head. "Oh, wow."

"Wait," Devin said. "Here comes the tragic part. He got permission to take me out of school all week so I can help out on the farm."

"Oh, noooo," I moaned.

"Oh, yes. So where am I going to be spending Halloween? In a pumpkin patch."

"No way. No way."

"Polly's party will be a total *thrill* by comparison," Devin said, shaking his head.

His hand scraped the bottom of the popcorn bowl. "Hey, what happened to all the popcorn?"

"Very funny. Most of it's stuck to your teeth."

I was joking around, but I felt bad for him. He's not a farm kind of guy. He actually spent his first seven years in New York City. Then his dad got transferred here to Dayton, Ohio.

But Devin is a city dude.

"You're just going to rot with the pumpkins," I said sadly.

He sighed. "Thanks for trying to cheer me up."

That made us both laugh. I checked the clock on the cable box. Then I jumped to my feet. "See you when you get back," I said. "Good luck." I gave him a hard, phony handshake.

He stood up. "Lu-Ann, where are you going?" he asked as I pushed him toward the front door.

"I have to go scare my little brother now."

I tell my brother, Mitch, a scary story every night before he goes to sleep. I just make them up as I go along.

Mitch likes my stories and he hates them at the same time. He doesn't really like to be scared. He grits his teeth and shuts his fists and pretends he's brave.

I don't want to torture the poor kid. But I only know how to tell scary stories. That's the only kind of story I can dream up. I guess I just have a scary mind.

Mitch and I look alike a little bit. We both have straight black hair and dark eyes and round faces. I'm very thin, but he's pretty chubby. Mom says he hasn't lost his baby fat.

How do you think that line goes over with Mitch?

Not too well.

Mitch is a quiet, serious kid. He's only eight, but he likes to read endlessly long fantasy books about ancient kingdoms and dragons and battles and stuff.

He gets straight A's at Meadowdale, his elementary school. But he doesn't have a lot of friends.

I think it's because he's so quiet and shy.

We get along great even though we're so different. The only thing we fight about is breakfast — toaster waffles or toaster pancakes? He goes for waffles, and I like the pancakes. Mom says it would be silly to buy both. So . . . big fights in the supermarket.

I took Mitch into the kitchen for his nightly bedtime snack — Oreos and a glass of milk to dip them in. Then we headed upstairs. Mitch climbed into his platform bed and pulled up the covers.

Dad got him a platform bed down on the floor because he tosses and turns and rolls around a lot at night. And he was always falling out of his old bed and hurting himself.

"What's the story about?" he asked, fluffing the pillow behind his head. "Don't make it too scary, okay?"

"Okay. Not too scary," I said. Total lie.

"Tonight's story is about an evil old man. The man was so evil, he could turn himself into a snarling, clawing monster. Just by concentrating on being evil."

"What's his name?"

"His name was Mitch," I said. "Stop interrupting."

"No. Really. What was his name?"

"His name was Evil Boris. But people just called him Evil. Everyone was afraid of him. Every night, Evil Boris would take a walk around town and do something evil."

"Like what?"

I had the bedroom lights turned low. Mitch's dark eyes glowed in the dim light, wide with fright. His hands gripped the top of the blanket. I told the story in a whisper, just to make it scarier.

"Evil Boris liked to step on cats. Some nights he picked up big, metal trash cans and poured garbage into people's cars. He crushed birds in his bare hands. He liked to smash windows on houses just to hear the crackling glass sound. And — and guess what else?"

"What else?" Mitch asked in a tiny voice.

"Once a week, he ate someone."

"He ate people?" Mitch asked.

"He only ate kids, about your age," I said.

I almost laughed. I love making up these stories. And it makes me happy when I can think of creepy ideas like that.

"He liked to taste them first. Maybe he'd start by chewing on an arm. Sometimes he started with a leg. But the strange thing is . . . Evil Boris always saved the head for last."

Mitch made a gulping sound.

"Can you picture it?" I whispered. "Can you picture Evil Boris turning himself into a fanged monster and pulling apart someone your age . . . chewing . . . chewing . . . chewing and swallowing."

"Stop, Lu-Ann," Mitch begged. "I don't want to picture it. You said you wouldn't make it too scary."

"But I didn't tell you the scary part," I whispered. "Don't you want to hear the scary part?"

"No!" Mitch shouted. "No, I don't."

"The scary part is . . . Evil Boris lives in your closet, Mitch. He lives in the back of your clothes closet."

"Noooo!"

Uh-oh. I think I went too far. Mitch was starting to lose it.

I could see the bedcovers trembling. And I saw the dark glow of his wide, frightened eyes.

"Mitch," I said softly. I patted his shoulder. "It's just a story. It isn't true." I smoothed a hand through his thick, dark hair. "I made the whole thing up. Don't be afraid."

"Too scary," he murmured. His eyes were on the clothes closet across the bedroom.

"Go ahead. Check out the closet," I said. I tugged him up. "Go look in the closet. You'll see. It's empty. There's no one in there."

He pulled back. "I don't want to."

"It's just a story," I said. "Quick. Go look in the closet. Prove it to yourself. Then you can go to sleep."

He climbed slowly to his feet. His eyes were locked on the closet door. He crossed the room to the closet.

"Go ahead. Open it," I urged. "You'll see. No one there."

Mitch grabbed the door handle. He pulled open the door — and a hideous old man with long curled fangs and a dangling eyeball came roaring out at him.

Mitch opened his mouth in a shriek of horror.

I clapped my hands to my face. "My story!" I cried. "It *came true!*"

About the Author

R.L. Stine's books are read all over the world. So far, his books have sold more than 300 million copies, making him one of the most popular children's authors in history. Besides Goosebumps, R.L. Stine has written the teen series Fear Street and the funny series Rotten School, as well as the Mostly Ghostly series, The Nightmare Room series, and the two-book thriller *Dangerous Girls*. R.L. Stine lives in New York with his wife, Jane, and Minnie, his King Charles spaniel. You can learn more about him at www.RLStine.com.

DOUBLE THE FRIGHT
ALL AT ONE SITE
www.scholastic.com/goosebumps

FIENDS OF GOOSEBUMPS &
GOOSEBUMPS HORRORLAND CAN:

- PLAY GHOULISH GAMES!

- CHAT WITH FELLOW FAN-ATICS!

- WATCH CLIPS FROM SPINE-TINGLING DVDs!

- EXPLORE CLASSIC BOOKS AND NEW TERROR-IFIC TITLES!

- CHECK OUT THE GOOSEBUMPS HORRORLAND VIDEO GAME!

- GET GOOSEBUMPS PHOTOSHOCK FOR THE iPHONE™ OR iPOD TOUCH®!

SCHOLASTIC

GBWEB

The Original Bone-Chilling Series

—with Exclusive
Author Interviews!

R. L. Stine's Fright Fest!
Now with Splat Stats and More!

THE SCARIEST PLACE ON EARTH!

GOOSEBUMPS® HALL OF HORRORS

THERE'S ALWAYS ROOM FOR ONE MORE SCREAM!

An all-new series from fright-master R.L. Stine!